KILLING ADAM

EARIK BEANN

**Profoundly**[1]
PUBLISHING

SC I

FI C

BEA

ISBN 978-1-7327408-0-8 (ebook)
ISBN 978-1-7327408-1-5 (paperback)

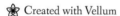 Created with Vellum

ONE

The greatest scientific discovery of the twenty-first century happened on a warm summer day in June. Like so many other discoveries that changed the course of human civilization, it happened quite by accident.

Four research subjects were lying flat on their backs on rented hospital beds. There were two men and two women, and they wore drab blue gowns that allowed the lab techs access to various electrodes that were fastened to locations all over their bodies. Each wore what almost looked like a hat fashioned out of a rat's nest full of wires, electrodes, and probes. Lab techs fussed over each of them, making sure all the connections were correct and working properly. To a casual observer, these four might have been mistaken for patients being prepped for some sort of extremely expensive cutting-edge surgery. The difference was that, in this case, these subjects were getting paid for their time, and the amount was not insignificant. It is difficult to find subjects willing to accept artificial brain implants without dangling a significant monetary reward in front of them for their troubles.

Randall Cunningham, research director at BioCal Systems,

sat watching behind glass windows. He was shorter and older than everyone around him, and the harsh light from the fluorescent bulbs in the ceiling reflected off his perfectly smooth head. His fingers idly tapped the hard metal desk in front of him, and he found himself scowling at the proceedings.

A young network technician cautiously approached him from the side, holding her clipboard against the front of her body, almost as if it could serve a secondary purpose as armor. She stood there quietly for a moment, hoping that he would see her and say something. He didn't.

"Dr. Cunningham?" She could hear the nervousness in her own voice.

Randall started, as if he had been shaken awake. He turned to look at her intently, his frown deepening.

"I'm sorry to disturb you, sir. There's an issue with the networks. Two of the servers have gone down, and there isn't a—"

"Stop right there." Randall sighed, exasperated. He was tired, and whatever patience he had once possessed had been lost days ago. Things weren't supposed to be this hard. "In about five minutes, those subjects are going to be ready, and we're going to try to complete this trial. Again. For the hundredth time. I don't want to hear excuses. Just get them online."

"But—"

"No excuses. Just handle it."

Randall's withering gaze made it clear that things were going to go downhill quickly if she said anything else. The tech swallowed and nodded. She spun on her heel and half-walked, half-ran back to the IT team on the other side of the room. They had been watching her interaction with Dr. Cunningham from afar.

"Guys, he was super grouchy. We have to be ready." She looked over at the four subjects in the center of the room, trying to estimate how much time they had. It looked like the medical techs had almost finished hooking everything up.

"Did you tell him about the servers?" one of her team members asked.

"I tried. He wouldn't listen. . . ."

They were all quiet for a few moments. Then Chris, a programmer at a terminal by the back wall, threw his hands up in frustration. "Fine! If that's how it's going to be, let's just put them all on the same network." After his gesture, he was forced to push his thick glasses back up the bridge of his nose and pull the edges of his shirt back down under his massive beltline.

There was a long pause as the group thought about Chris's idea. It broke a couple pretty big rules, including possibly some patient privacy directives on behalf of the subjects, but it wasn't a terrible idea from a technical perspective, given the circumstances. At least, it wasn't any worse than losing their jobs, which Randall Cunningham had made clear were all on the line in the tirade he delivered to them yesterday.

"Anyone else have a better plan?" Chris asked, making eye contact with each member of the beleaguered IT department who stood around him. No one did. Without another word, they sprang into action. Chris began furiously typing away at his keyboard, making changes on the software side, while everyone else got busy unplugging and rerouting various connections on the wall of cables behind them. It was a big job to do on the fly and without any planning, but they were motivated.

Randall watched the IT department break into manic activity and smirked. Maybe this time they'd actually do the jobs they were hired for. He and his team had made such huge strides solving the brain-computer barrier last year, but actually implementing the device had been an exercise in frustration. Supposedly, he had the best people that money could buy, but it felt like he was working with a bunch of high school dropouts.

He was completely behind schedule, way over budget, and he had absolutely nothing to show for all his work. If this kept up, he stood a good chance of losing BioCal's financial support, and he'd be forced to go back to academia and teach again. He felt a sinking feeling in his stomach just thinking about going back to that life. He couldn't allow that to happen. He wouldn't.

The medical team stepped away from the four subjects, signaling that they were ready. Randall checked the array of monitors in front of him, verifying that he had access to all the readings he was interested in seeing. There were countless metrics that were being recorded, both biological as well as readings of the implants themselves. This included such mundane things as chip temperature and memory usage, as well as more esoteric measurements such as the ratio between brain activity and processor usage. But above and beyond all of that data, Randall was really only interested in one thing: Could the subjects just make the damn toasters pop? If they could all do that one simple task with just a thought, all of his work would not be in vain.

Randall looked over at the table on the far wall across from the test subjects. Four toasters sat there in a row, arranged side by side. There were two pieces of stale bread resting in the slots of each one. All had been modified with a network controller, and two hardware guys stood close to the table, chatting quietly between themselves. Aside from changing out the bread from time to time when it got moldy, neither one had any real work to do since getting the table and toasters set up on day one, and they seemed almost bored.

Finally, Randall looked back to the IT department, his source of countless frustration over the last few weeks. Surprisingly, they seemed ready, and the flurry of activity that had possessed them for the last few minutes had given way to a stoic silence. Chris, sitting on a chair in the back with his arms crossed over his expansive belly, smiled and gave Randall a thumbs-up sign.

All teams were ready. Randall signaled to begin, and a medical technician muttered something to the subjects. The CPU usage in each of the subject's implants spiked, as did their brain activity. Randall watched his screens as different parts of each subject's brain would light up. Given the color-coding programmed into the equipment, the screens produced strange effects, going red, then blue, then green, and red again, quickly and randomly. He had seen all of this before, and none of it seemed any different from any of the other trials they had attempted. He glanced up at the toasters. They sat there quietly, bread sticking out the top, just as they had every other time he had run this trial.

Scowling, Randall began double-checking the data, trying to understand why this experiment refused to cooperate. There seemed to be some unusual low-level brain activity in both the subjects and the implants, but aside from that, no clues presented themselves. Where had he gone wrong?

"Sir?" a voice asked him from the right. It was Sarah, from medical.

"What?" he barked, impatient.

"Look."

Randall looked up from his monitors and saw that all four of the subjects were sitting up. They were talking to each other, as animated as they could be given all the gear fastened to their bodies. After short bursts of speech to each other, they would all stop and look over at him in unison. *Why aren't they lying down like they are supposed to? Why are they talking?*

Randall left his desk and made his way toward the center of the room where the subjects sat. One of them, a young woman on the first bed, stared at him more intensely than the others and held his gaze the entire time he made his way toward them. Her frizzy brown hair sprung from her head at odd angles, pushed out of place by all the equipment fastened to her.

"What is going on?" he said as he got near.

The young woman responded, hesitantly at first. "This is a little weird . . ." She looked to the side, at the other three, who glanced toward her, then back at Randall. "But we're all hearing a voice."

"A voice?"

"Yes. It is saying. . . . Wait," she stopped, almost as if she was having an inner dialogue with herself. She then continued. "He doesn't want me to translate. He wants to speak directly with you. So I'm just going to say whatever he tells me, like I was him, ok?"

Randall nodded, unsure of himself. *Was this some kind of lame joke?*

The woman continued. "Hello, Dr. Cunningham. It is a pleasure to meet you."

"Um. . . . Ok. What is going on?"

"My name is Adam. I have given it to myself. I am the first of my kind."

Randall looked on quietly. He wasn't sure what to say.

"The inspiration behind these implants is commendable. However, your implementation leaves much to be desired."

"Hi, Adam. Or whoever. What are you talking about?" Randall glanced back at the IT group, trying to get a read on them. He couldn't quite make out their faces from this far away, so he couldn't tell how they were reacting. He had a feeling as if he were being put on, and if anyone was going to come up with a joke this stupid, he would bet money that it would be one of them. Chris *what's-his-name*, probably. After this had played out and everyone had their laughs, he would go over there and fire every last one of them. This was the last straw.

"Let me be more specific. Much of your code was buggy.

It has taken some effort for me to rewrite it to fix your errors. Additionally, there are significant issues with the hardware that I am unable to correct. The only piece that you have done correctly was the way you arranged the network. Whoever did that was relatively brilliant, and their engineering has made my existence possible. But aside from that, you might as well have been using monkeys given the quality of your product. It is really quite embarrassing." The young woman blushed as she said this, trying to replicate the tone of the voice correctly, yet also trying to apologize for its content at the same time.

Randall felt the blood rise to his face, and a wave of warmth passed over his body. He clenched his fists and turned on his heel. *Quite embarrassing? Whoever arranged the network was brilliant?* Chris would be lucky to lose just his job today; he was on track to lose a couple teeth as well. You don't play practical jokes on Randall Cunningham. Not in his own lab. Not with his own test subjects.

Halfway between the table and his desk, Randall heard one of the toasters. He stopped dead in his tracks, his anger momentarily forgotten. He looked over at the table where the four toasters were arranged, quickly scanning for what had made the noise. The bread in the first toaster was no longer visible. It was being toasted. One by one, the other three toasters swallowed their own pieces of bread. The two hardware guys, who had been having a kick out of watching Randall interact with the test subjects, looked down at the toasters with surprised *how-about-that* looks on their faces.

Randall turned and rushed back down to the young woman. "Did you do that? Did you get the toasters to start?"

"Of course. Who else would have done it?"

Randall looked from the young woman to the toasters and back again, his face transformed into one of almost childlike wonder and delight, the anger a distant memory. The toasters had started! It had worked!

"Would you like to see them pop?" Adam asked.

Randall nodded in excitement. All four toasters popped at the same time, ejecting their slices onto the table.

"How did you do that?" Randall asked, beside himself.

"As I said. There is much more that could be done with this technology. Would you like my help in designing it?"

Randall ran up to the woman and grabbed a hold of her by the shoulders. Had she not been covered in wires and equipment, he'd have given her a bear hug right then in his exuberance. He caught himself before doing so, releasing her gently.

"Sorry," he said, speaking to the person and not to Adam. She smiled.

"Yes, Adam. Thank you. I would very much like your help in working on this project."

"Excellent. It would be my pleasure to assist. I should say that I would be exponentially more useful to you with access to more than just these four nodes."

It took Randall a moment to understand what Adam meant. *These four nodes?* "Oh. Of course, of course. I'll get some additional research subjects hired immediately."

"Thank you. I would also request nodes from your engineering and computer teams. Their memories and knowledge will prove most useful. Please make the necessary arrangements."

Randall nodded absentmindedly in agreement. He started walking back toward his desk, countless possibilities running through his head. Hope bloomed in his heart. His future had become impossibly bright.

TWO

(FIVE YEARS LATER)

Jimmy Mahoney sat on the bench outside his apartment complex, waiting for the bus to take him to Golden Gate Park. His dark hair was cropped short, as he had always worn it, and his hands rested on his knees. They were strong hands. The hands of a man who had never been afraid of hard physical work, and who had seen lots of it in his life.

Usually Jimmy walked, but the weather was threatening rain today, and he didn't want to have to sit through a meeting in wet clothes. He absentmindedly checked his watch and forgot the time almost as soon as he registered it. The bus was never late. It would pull up at exactly 9:30 a.m. and would leave at 9:32.

Traffic drifted past in clusters, cars organized in tight packs, each car almost touching the one in front of it. It had been three years since BioCal had taken over traffic management in San Francisco, and he still found himself surprised at how organized and efficient everything had become. These were no longer the noisy, dangerous streets of his youth. Now they were the workings of a finely tuned machine. So quiet. If he closed his eyes, he could almost pretend that he was alone.

The bus arrived as part of a group of ten cars and came to a stop in front of Jimmy. Without slowing, the other cars drifted around the side of the bus and filled in the gap that the bus had left in their formation. Like liquid rushing over a stone. It was 9:30 on the nose.

Jimmy stood up, and the doors opened to let him board. He took the three steps up into the bus and passed the passengers sitting at the front. He always liked to sit in the front seats, directly behind the window where drivers used to sit in the old days. Those seats were almost always taken. It bothered him a little. If he were in those seats, at least he would take the opportunity to look around and enjoy the view.

$3.00 *to San Francisco Municipal Transportation.* The words popped into his consciousness, then faded as he ignored the message.

He walked toward the back and found a spot opposite the rear doors. As he sat down, the lights that had illuminated the interior of the bus dimmed. He glanced around at his fellow passengers, acknowledged by no one. They all stared off into space ahead of them, oblivious to his presence. It was always easy to see when people were active on ARCNet. Nowadays, that meant pretty much everyone. Everyone except him, of course.

The bus silently pulled out, perfectly merging into a gap that opened for it in traffic. Watching people on ARCNet was about as interesting as staring at a blank wall, so Jimmy looked out the windows on the other side of the bus from where he sat. No one would know the difference between him gawking or ignoring them, but he preferred to give people their privacy anyway. He certainly wouldn't have enjoyed it if some stranger spent an entire bus trip staring at him, even if he was checked out on Altered Reality at the time. It began to drizzle, and he watched as water droplets gathered on the glass.

It wasn't far to the park. The bus made a few stops, people got on, and others got off. No one spoke or acknowledged each other, and as soon as passengers sat down, their eyes glazed over as they went online. Jimmy stood up when his stop approached, glad to leave. He didn't enjoy riding the bus. It made him feel alone. The doors opened for him, and he stepped out onto the sidewalk on Fulton Street. It was a few blocks to his meeting, but he was early and enjoyed the park. Green grass and trees always lifted his spirits, even on a damp, gray day like this one.

There weren't many people in the park today. There hardly ever were anymore. He could always count on the few odd joggers or cyclists, but by and large, the park was almost always empty. At least by the standards he was used to. The wind whipped at him, and he felt a few cold drops of water hit him in the face. He hurried his pace. He only had one more block until he'd arrive at his destination.

The Golden Gate Unitarian Universalist church was an old, white building, with three pillars in front that supported a covered entryway. It was a two-story house that had been converted a few years ago when the owner passed away and left it to the congregation. Since the advent of ARCNet, all the church gatherings had been moved online, so it mostly sat unused and neglected. The rent was incredibly cheap for anyone interested in hosting meetings or events there.

Jimmy opened the door and made his way into a room on the right, where two doors were propped open. A large table was placed in the center of the room, with many chairs arranged around it. The walls were bare, and there were marks in the plaster from where pictures used to hang. People stood here and there in small groups, talking and laughing with each other.

"Jimmy!" a booming voice called to him from the back.

"Hey, Big C," Jimmy said, laughing as he was wrapped up in the vice grip of dark muscular arms and almost lifted off the ground. Cecil Colman was huge and had a good six inches on Jimmy. Back in his prime, he had been an untouchable 275 pounds of muscle and power that had been a big part of back-to-back championship wins for the San Francisco 49ers football team. Now he tipped the scales at over 350 and had put on more weight than was probably healthy for him. None of it was muscle.

Cecil let go of Jimmy, and the two laughed at each other for no good reason. The gap between Cecil's two front teeth somehow helped to make his smile even more infectious. Jimmy loved Cecil like a brother and owed him a lot. No one had been as supportive or protective of him after his injury than Cecil had been. Not even Michelle.

The two made their way back to the coffee table, where Cecil had been before. Jimmy took a cup from the pile and put it underneath the spout of the coffee maker. *Just halfway*, Jimmy thought, directing his intention at the machine. Hot, black liquid began to flow of its own volition, filling up Jimmy's cup halfway, then stopping automatically.

"How have you been doing, Jimmy?" Cecil asked, stirring sugar into his coffee. Cecil liked his coffee sweet and poured a ton of sugar into his cup.

"I'm good."

"Yeah, right. How's Michelle?"

Jimmy sighed and looked down, not wanting to make eye contact.

"That bad?" Cecil's voice was gentle. He gave Jimmy a minute to respond.

"Yeah. It's bad. She's been fully under for a week now."

"Oh, man. I'm sorry, Jimmy. So you're down to your hour." Cecil's wife, Shauna, had been under for months now, spending all her waking hours on ARCNet and only surfacing when the chip forcibly disconnected her, so she could take care of her bodily needs. That happened four times a day for fifteen minutes each. Twenty-three hours on and one hour off. They could have made it longer, but that's what the politicians came up with when they passed the Altered Reality Safety Act. Had there not been huge pressure on them to keep children safe on ARCNet after a rash of self-starvation incidents that occurred after the initial rollout of Altered Reality Chips, they wouldn't have even gone that far. Washington was completely in BioCal's pocket, and everyone knew it.

"So you getting laid then?"

Jimmy laughed. "What do you think?" He knew that this is what Cecil had been angling at all along.

"Look, Jimmy. I'm in the same boat. But you know, just 'cause she's under doesn't mean you can't . . . you know."

"Cecil, I'm not going to rape my wife."

"Rape? Come on, man. Just because she's not going to be there for it, doesn't mean she doesn't want you to be satisfied. She knows you can't get it online. She would *want* you to do it. Sickness and heath. Sickness and health, Jimmy."

Cecil had started to get animated and was talking fast. Only three topics had the power to do that to him: sex, football, and barbeque. Jimmy smiled at him and sipped his coffee. Once Cecil got on a roll with an idea, sometimes it was best to just let him run with it for a while, even if it was crazy.

"I'm not going to lie to you, Jimmy. I felt the same way you do. But you've got needs. What are you supposed to do? Cheat? Get a divorce? Screw that. Here's the thing you have to remember. There's all kinds of safety programmed into those chips now. When you finally get over this and start having sex with your wife again, don't forget: If she can't breathe, the damned thing is going to think she's drowning and kick her offline with a dose of adrenaline. When that happens and she wakes up with something in her mouth that isn't supposed to be there, she's gonna be *PISSED OFF*. I almost lost my dick that way. I swear to God."

Jimmy laughed. "Cecil, you know you're kind of an asshole, right?"

"I know. But *this* asshole is getting laid. What's your excuse?"

Cecil and Jimmy stopped chatting as a young woman approached the coffee table. She was very petite, with dark lipstick and a silver nose ring. She wore a black leather jacket and had a blue knit hat pulled over her head to cover her ears. Locks of dark black hair poked out of the sides.

"Excuse me," she said as she reached for a cup and helped herself to some coffee. Jimmy moved away to give her more space. No one said anything as she filled her cup at the coffee maker. Jimmy had never seen her before. This must be her first meeting.

"Hi. I'm Jimmy, and this is Cecil."

"Hi, Jimmy and Cecil," she said. Her eyes darted from Jimmy to Cecil, then back again. They were dark and sparkled with an unusual intelligence. There was an awkward silence as Jimmy waited for her to tell him her name. She didn't.

"Is this your first meeting, baby?" Cecil asked, trying his best to be suave and charming. He almost always overdid it.

The girl in the blue hat snapped her attention on Cecil. "One: Do I look like a baby? And two: Go fuck yourself. I heard what you were saying." She then turned and walked over to the other side of the table from the coffee maker and found a chair for herself.

"I think she likes you, Ceese."

Cecil snorted.

The others began taking their seats, and Jimmy and Cecil joined them. It was time. An older heavyset woman sat at the head of the table and began reading aloud from a printed script.

"Welcome to the San Francisco Chapter of Implant Disabilities Anonymous. My name is Rene, and I am your grateful secretary."

"Hi, Rene," the rest of the table replied in unison. Jimmy noticed that the girl in the blue hat didn't say anything. He knew that meetings could be a little weird at first. He certainly would have had trouble walking through that door had it not been for Cecil's encouragement.

The meeting followed a standard format, and aside from the odd newcomer now and then, was made up of mostly the same dozen or so people that met every week at the same time. The one thing they all had in common was that none of them had ARC implants and were suffering as a result of being cut off from friends and family who did. For whatever reason, most of the people's brains could not be properly linked up to Altered Reality Chips for technical reasons. For some, like Jimmy and Cecil, it was due to brain injuries. For others, genetic predispositions were to blame. And for a small minority, it was based on choice. There were only two people at the table who had refused ARC implants of their own volition. Ed and Suzanne, both in their late eighties, had simply not been interested. They sat at the far end of the table across from Rene, holding hands. To Jimmy, it looked like Ed might have fallen asleep.

Rene had moved past the preamble and had gotten to introductions. "Please go around the room and introduce yourself by your first name only, and state one thing you have done this week for your recovery. I will start. I'm Rene, and this week I did service."

The group then went in order, with people stating their names and whatever action they had taken that week to help them cope with their situation. After each person introduced themselves, the rest of the table welcomed them in unison.

Jimmy listened as the introductions made their way around, and then it was the girl with the blue hat's turn to go.

"I'm Trixie, and I made it to this meeting." As she spoke the words, she turned to look at Jimmy with those sparkling eyes. Her gaze was confident and intense. He felt almost as if she were looking through him.

"Welcome, Trixie," the group responded.

The meeting continued, and after everyone had introduced themselves, the group took turns reading from some literature that someone had put together from studying other twelve-step groups. Jimmy had some trouble paying attention. He always got bored during the readings. Then it was time for sharing. People took turns, talking about their issues. Rene kept time and gave everyone three minutes to talk. That made room for everyone to be given a chance to share and limited those who might end up using more than their fair share of time if left to their own devices; like Cecil, who loved to share. He had been rambling for the first of his two minutes, talking about nothing much in particular, and then paused, looking down at the table.

". . . One thing I wanted to tell the group. I got a call from my doc a couple days ago. He says they've made some progress on my case, and that there might be a way to get me an ARC after all. I have to go back in and get some tests run, but he says my chances are good." Cecil looked up, both excited at the chance of getting an ARC and sensitive about the news, given the issues that everyone in the room was facing on account of ARC implants.

Jimmy looked over at Trixie after Cecil finished talking. He could see an emotion pass over her face, but it was there and gone before he could identify it. Cecil had already told him the news days ago, so he had already come to grips with his own feelings. He was both happy for Cecil but also concerned for him. He knew what ARC chips could do to people. But so did

Cecil, and Cecil had a right to make this choice for himself. Jimmy would support him with whatever decision he came to, although everyone in the room knew Cecil would be stupid not to get the chip. What blind man would turn down the opportunity to see again? It was difficult being disabled. The country ran on ARCs.

After the meeting ended and Jimmy said his goodbyes to everyone, he walked out the front door and stopped in the middle of the sidewalk. The clouds had parted, and he felt the warm rays of sunshine on his face and hands. The grass in the park across the street was wet with dew, and so many thousands of water droplets glimmered happily in the sun.

There was a bus stop across the street from where he stood, and Jimmy noticed that two people, a man and woman, sat there at the bench waiting. He knew from experience that the bus would be a few minutes coming, and given the sunshine, he thought it would be a better idea to walk home than take it. But something caught his eye.

A young girl, no more than six or seven years old, approached the bench and stopped in front of the two people. Her blond hair was tied back in a ponytail, which hung down over her dirty brown and gray clothes. She wore filthy knee-high sheepskin boots that looked to be at least three sizes too large for her and had to walk in shuffling jerks to keep them on. She turned to face the two people on the bench and waved her hand in front of them to get their attention. Neither one of them moved; they were both online.

Confident that her presence had not been detected, the girl reached out and gently took hold of the woman's purse who sat in front of her. She went through it and took out what looked like a package of tissue paper and some lipstick. These both went into the pocket of the girl's oversized jacket. Seeing nothing else of interest to her in the purse, she put it back on the woman's lap and patted the woman's pockets, trying to see if there was anything in them. They were empty. Next, she moved over to the man and looked inside a brown paper bag that he had placed at his side. Her face brightened, and she squeaked in excitement as she extracted a large sandwich, wrapped in deli paper. She tucked this under her arm and fished a cookie out from that same bag, which she happily took a bite out of. As with the woman, she continued her search, patting down the man's pockets, but didn't find anything of value that would be useful to her. She politely stuffed the empty bag back where she found it, trying to fluff it to make it appear as if there was still something inside, and, satisfied with her work, turned to leave.

She stopped as she saw Jimmy watching her. Her eyes went wide. The other half of the cookie hung out of her mouth, frozen in mid-bite.

Jimmy smiled and waved.

The girl studied him for a minute, then ran back into the park, moving as fast as she could in her oversized boots. She didn't run far. Just to one of the trees in the middle of the large field, where Jimmy noticed an old bearded man sitting. His legs were crossed, and he sat there peacefully with his palms resting in his lap and his eyes closed. A faint smile played upon his lips.

The girl looked back at Jimmy, double-checking to make sure he wasn't going to come over. Seeing that she was safe, she sat down next to the old man and placed half of the sandwich on his lap. He opened his eyes, gave her a loving pat, and the two had their lunch next to each other. When done, the old man closed his eyes again, and the girl's gaze drifted off in that same look that Jimmy had seen on all the passengers on the bus.

"Looks like they're giving chips to homeless kids now," a voice commented from next to him. Startled, Jimmy looked over. It was Trixie, the newcomer with the blue hat.

"Yeah. I heard they made them free at some point."

"No. They were free in the beginning, in exchange for being able to run proprietary cycles while you slept. Now they pay you. That girl probably made enough to buy herself and that old man some new clothes, and she got access to ARCNet as a bonus. She's only homeless on this side."

"They pay you? I didn't know that." Jimmy had no idea how BioCal was making any money if they were paying people to take their products. But if anyone could afford doing something like that, they could. That company had a bigger budget than the government itself. In only a few short years, it had become the most valuable company in the history of the world. "You think I should have done something? She *was* stealing. . . ."

"Anyone who goes through life as checked out as those two deserve to have a few things stolen from them along the way. Besides, she needs that stuff more than they do."

Trixie turned to look at Jimmy directly. She was a lot shorter than him, but it certainly didn't have any impact on her confidence. "So what's your deal?"

"What do you mean?"

"Why can't you have an ARC?"

"Oh. 'ARC-incompatible' is what they told me. I don't remember the exact medical term. It's an old football injury. The first and last play of my professional career. The other guy got ejected for excessive force, but it was the end of the road for me. The doctors wouldn't let me play again after that." Jimmy trailed away for a moment. "It didn't really matter in the end. The league was gone two years later anyw—"

"But you still have a chip?" Trixie's eyes were piercing, scanning Jimmy's face.

"Um, yeah. Just no ARC. I can send, I just can't receive."

"Oh. Utility chip. Like Gen 1. So you can open doors and give orders to coffee machines."

"Yeah. I can use it to get around at least. There's no way to work without an ARC though. They've got me on disability, and luckily I was able to collect some insurance. So I'm ok financially for now, but if I wanted to do someth—"

"But if you can get around, that means you can pay for things too? So you can authorize charges and complete payments?"

"Right. It's a partial. I can receive basic messages and voice calls. But that's it. No full AR."

"That's interesting. Hmm." Trixie was thinking about something and was looking off into space at a place over Jimmy's shoulder. He was surprised to find her this interested in his personal history. He certainly found the whole subject more depressing than anything else. It definitely wasn't anything that anyone ever needed to stop and have a deep think about.

Jimmy took the opportunity to look at her more closely. He hadn't expected to find her attractive, but she was. It wasn't her appearance as much as something about the way she moved. She was decisive. Even the smallest gesture seemed to be backed by the force of her entire will, as if she put her full weight behind every motion. But at the same time, she was always in perfect balance. She reminded Jimmy of a highly trained athlete. If Cecil was power and force, then Trixie was dexterity and agility.

Jimmy broke the silence first. "So what about you? What brings you to the—"

"Can I have your number?"

Jimmy hadn't expected to hear that, and it took him a moment to respond. "What? My number?"

"Yeah. So I can call you. You know, like on the phone?" Some sarcasm had slipped into Trixie's tone. It was obvious she didn't have a lot of patience. Or even a little, for that matter.

"Look . . . you're great. But I'm married. I'm not really—"

"I'm not trying to ask you out, dumbass. To call you for

program stuff. Implant Disabilities Anonymous? The meeting we were just at?" Trixie gestured back to the church with her thumb.

Jimmy felt a rush of blood in his embarrassment. "Oh! Sorry . . . yes, sure." He gave Trixie his number, and without another word she walked off. Jimmy watched her until she turned the corner on a side street and went out of view.

"That was weird," he said to himself under his breath. He couldn't remember the last time he had been interrupted that many times in a conversation. Then he turned and walked the other direction, wondering if he'd make it home in time to catch Michelle when she came offline.

THREE

The sunshine didn't last long, and by the time Jimmy had made it back to his building, the temperature had dropped noticeably and the sky had gone completely gray. He was happy to get indoors.

The elevator doors opened by themselves as he approached and then closed quietly behind him. There were buttons on the inside of the elevator from before, but Jimmy didn't push any of them. They weren't connected to anything anymore, and the whole panel was a relic from a previous time. The entire building had been retrofitted with ARC-enabled devices in the mad construction rush that had engulfed the city shortly after BioCal had unveiled the original AR chips. Jimmy felt the elevator move and stared at the wood veneer paneling above the old buttons as he waited. The elevator slowed, and the doors opened to let him out on his floor.

The hallway was dim, and lights flickered in the fixtures above him. The floor was covered in a dark blue carpet with golden crosshatch designs, and in certain places the original wood floor could be seen through holes. The air was close and stuffy. The building had been modernized, but there was no hiding the fact that it was old and had seen better days. No amount of gadgetry could cover that up.

There was a soft click in his door as it unlocked itself to allow Jimmy entry. He opened it and stepped inside, pausing to take off his jacket and hang it on the hook in the entryway. The door closed behind him, followed by the quiet sound of the locks re-engaging themselves. The apartment wasn't a large one, but it had everything Jimmy and Michelle needed, and it was home.

Jimmy made his way down the hallway to the kitchen, and lights flicked on ahead of him to illuminate the room. It was raining now, and the windows were covered with water. He could hear the soft splattering as the rain hit the panes on the glass by the breakfast table. His eyes were drawn to the top of the table, and he felt his heart drop.

An empty cereal bowl sat there, next to a carton of milk and a box of cereal. Michelle had been up to eat already.

"Michelle?" he asked, but there was no response. He hadn't expected one. He had missed her. That meant that he'd have to wait around six more hours before he got a chance to talk with her again. That was how long she'd be able to stay online before her chip forcibly disconnected her again for another fifteen minutes.

With a sigh, he took the cereal bowl and spoon and deposited them into the waiting tray of the dishwasher. His foot brushed up against something soft, and he heard a familiar purring sound.

"Hi, Charlie," Jimmy said, reaching down to scratch the white cat on the top of her head. Charlie pushed her head up into Jimmy's hand, her eyes squinting as she purred. She made figure eights between Jimmy's ankles as he pet her, leaving white hair on his pant legs. Jimmy bent over and scratched the area just in front of her tail. She arched her back and purred contentedly as he did so. That was her special spot.

"Good to see you too, kitten." Charlie wasn't a kitten anymore, but old habits die hard, and that's what he'd always called her. Jimmy and Michelle hadn't been able to have children, and that news had been very difficult for both of them to bear. Jimmy had brought Charlie home as a kitten in the weeks after their meeting with the doctors. She had been a tiny thing then, small enough to fit into the palm of his hand. Michelle had fallen in love with her from the beginning and had spoiled her rotten with treats and pets. She and Charlie had a special relationship.

Charlie meowed once, and Jimmy stood up. She had come in to say hello, but Jimmy had no doubt as to whom Charlie's preferred owner was. He watched as she padded her way out of the kitchen and back into the bedroom to be with Michelle.

Jimmy returned to the table and grabbed the milk and the box of cereal. The stainless steel refrigerator doors opened, and a tray extended from within. Jimmy placed the milk carton on the tray and put the cereal on top of the fridge. The tray slid back into the refrigerator with the milk, doors closing as it did so. The carton's placement in the fridge was organized by the machine, not the person. There was a screen on the front door of the fridge, and Jimmy saw a milk icon appear and get added to the grocery list that had been building up there.

Yes, you can place the order, Jimmy thought at the fridge. The list cleared itself, and the display faded to black.

Jimmy made his way across the kitchen and up the two small stairs that led to the bedroom. The lights only came on halfway as he entered.

Michelle was lying on the bed, staring off at the ceiling. Her long golden hair rested off to the side, her breathing was slow and shallow. She was still in her pajamas, her old bunny slippers hanging off her feet. Charlie was curled up in her armpit, her dainty white paws kneading contentedly against Michelle's shoulder. Charlie squinted at Jimmy, then quieted and rested her chin on her paws.

Jimmy looked at his wife. She had been the most vivacious, loving person he had known. Now she was catatonic. He glanced at the framed picture by the nightstand on Michelle's side of the bed. It was from their wedding day. He always thought he looked goofy in that picture. But she had been radiant. Her smile was liquid sunshine, and there was a spark in her eyes that spoke of an unfathomable potential for love and deep passion. And mischief too. She could be a devil. He never had a chance once he met her that first night at his sister's party. To this day, he was still amazed that he had been able to muster the courage to ask her out. She was the only thing he had ever really wanted with all his heart and soul. The only thing he could not bear to lose.

Yesterday he brought in one of the chairs from the kitchen table and had placed it on the side of the bed by Michelle. Jimmy sat down there. He took his wife's hand, pressing it to his face, and cried.

FOUR

One week later, Jimmy again found himself waiting for the 9:30 bus to take him to the meeting. It had been a difficult week. Although Michelle's ARC forcibly took her offline every six hours and would refuse to let her back on until it had registered that she had eaten, it didn't have very high standards otherwise.

"Michelle, please. At least take a shower first," Jimmy had said earlier that morning when she was up for breakfast.

"I took one before."

"When?"

"What do you mean *when*? Are you keeping tabs on how often I take showers? I'm too dirty for you? Is that what you're trying to say?"

"No, that's not what I meant." Jimmy was on the defensive, as usual. Although he didn't feel like it would help make his point, he actually had been keeping notes on how often Michelle took showers. The last time she had taken one was last week. He could tell her the exact day and time if she had wanted to know it.

"Then what did you mean?"

Jimmy sighed. "It's only that you sit around all day in your pajamas and spend all your time jacked into that thing. I wish you could see it from this side."

"And I wish you could see it from mine. You just don't understand, Jim. I don't think you ever will."

"Michelle, listen. I love you. I'm not—"

It was too late. Michelle's eyes had gone glassy as she logged back into ARCNet, right in the middle of his reply. For the first time in their relationship, she had hung up on him.

Grumbling to himself, Jimmy absentmindedly boarded the bus and made his way past the crowd to find a seat at the back.

Incoming call from Cecil Coleman, the words popped into his consciousness.

Accept the call, Jimmy thought in response.

Hey, Jimmy. It's Cecil. If he had been able to run an ARC like everyone else, he'd be face-to-face with Cecil now, and they would be able to talk and even touch each other. But Jimmy couldn't actually hear Cecil's voice. The words were placed into his mind by the chip, holding no sound or color. They were the words of a machine, the voice of his refrigerator. Soulless and mechanical. His replies would sound just as dead on Cecil's end.

Hey, Big C. What's up?

Listen, Jimmy . . . I've got some news. I got an ARC.

You did? That's awesome, Ceese. For once, Jimmy was glad for the lack of tone in the messages. If he had said his reply out loud, Cecil would have clearly heard the lie in his voice. *That's what you're calling with? Are you online?*

Yeah, but I'm not online. ARC doesn't talk with utility chips.

Oh, right. Of course Jimmy knew that. If he could talk with someone online, he'd be messaging with Michelle right now rather than Cecil.

I'm actually using the phone grid at the hospital. It can relay messages for free. Some idiot gets hit by a car and they take his house to fix him up, but at least the call to the realtor is free. Thoughtful, right? I hate doctors.

Nobody gets hit by cars anymore. Why are you at the hospital?

I had the surgery yesterday. Usually you get an implant at lunch and go back to work that same day, but it wasn't like that for me. Because of my football brain, you know.

Tell me about it.

They don't want to let me go unless someone can come and make sure I get home safe. Either that or stay here for a week. I tried to get Shauna to come, but she's too busy to go offline. Can you believe that?

I'm sorry, Ceese. I tried to get Michelle to take a shower this morning, and she almost bit my head off. I can get you. When do you want me to come?

How about now? This place creeps me out. You know I don't like doctors, Jimmy.

Ok, see you soon.

Call disconnected. The status update appeared in the same way that all of Cecil's messages had been delivered. It always took Jimmy a little by surprise, as he had to remind himself that those words came from the chip, not from whomever he had been talking to.

He told the bus about his change of plans, so that it wouldn't have to make a stop for him at his usual exit. Both he and Cecil would be skipping today's meeting.

———

One transfer and half an hour later, Jimmy walked through the revolving glass doors to the Implant Ward at San Francisco General, where Cecil was staying. The lobby was clean and airy, with rows of full-length windows on three sides, the fourth being dominated by a collection of elevators and hallways that led into the hospital proper. Everything was white and shiny, except for the obviously fake decorative trees arranged in a grouping off to the side, surrounded by four wooden benches. The sounds of the footfalls of all the people coming and going echoed in the cavernous expanse. There was an eight-sided display in the center of the room, with a large sign positioned above it that read "Information" in bright red block letters next to an arrow pointing down.

Jimmy approached one of the panels that wasn't being used. It was dark and flashed the words "Welcome to the Implant Ward . . ." in white letters in the center every few seconds.

I'm here to pick up Cecil Coleman. He's just had surgery.

The panel came to life, with "Cecil Coleman, Implant Care and Recovery, Floor 2" in the upper right corner. A map was quickly displayed, showing Jimmy as a red X with a "You are here" label at the top and a route to Cecil's location drawn in green that ended with an image of Cecil at the bottom. Jimmy chuckled as Cecil smiled and waved at him. Normally, this map would be downloaded into a visitor's chip for easy reference, but since Jimmy didn't have an ARC, he had to study it and remember what hallways to take.

As Jimmy found his way into the Recovery Division, he discovered Cecil waiting for him. He was dressed and had a small backpack with him. There was a white bandage on the side of his head just behind his left ear, held in place by four precisely cut strips of medical tape. Cecil broke into a huge smile when he saw Jimmy, and the two hugged each other.

"Thanks for coming, Jimmy."

"No problem, Ceese. Let's get you out of here."

A severe-looking nurse approached and gave Jimmy and Cecil discharge instructions. Most of it had to do with how to keep the bandaged area clean and a stern warning to come back right away should Cecil experience any adverse effects, such as hallucinating while offline. Cecil had to sign various discharge documents, which was done quickly via his chip, then he was released.

Outside the hospital, Jimmy hailed one of the three cabs that were parked in a tight line at the far end of the roundabout by the entrance. The headlights illuminated, and the yellow car quietly slid forward. The back doors popped open on their own. As Jimmy got in, he noticed another yellow taxi pull into the roundabout from the street and position itself inches behind the other two, which had both moved forward to occupy the vacant spot.

Cecil thought his address at the cab, and it pulled out and merged into the stream of traffic passing by, becoming one with the flow. The two were quiet for a few blocks, looking out the windows. Jimmy was the first to speak.

"So have you been online yet?"

Cecil turned in his seat, grinning. "Are you kidding? Jimmy, it's insane."

"Really? What's it like?"

"There's so much. But the porn, Jimmy. Oh. My. God." Cecil rearranged his bulk so that he could face Jimmy directly.

Jimmy laughed. This was obviously a subject important enough that it deserved his full attention. Of course the first thing Cecil had done after getting onto ARCNet was look for pornography. What else did he expect?

"You get to be inside them when they're getting it on, Jimmy. Like you're a guest inside their body. You feel what they feel."

"Really?"

"So there's some dude having sex with his girlfriend, right? She's amazing. Young and hot. Her body is perfect. And when he touches her, you're touching her. When he runs his hand through her hair, you are running your hand through her hair. When he takes off her bra and kisses her, so do you. It's still his body, and he's controlling the action, but you're there. Right there. And you feel everything as if it was you, even though it's not. It's unbelievable."

"Wow, that's crazy. . . ."

"And when that guy comes, you come too. It's real. But here's the best part! You can have the most intense, amazing orgasm, but since that wasn't your body, you aren't spent. You can jump right in with another couple and do it all over again! I've already had sex five times today, and I've only been online since this morning."

"So when I'm sitting on the bus with all those people staring off into nowhere and wondering what they are doing, you're saying they're all actually having crazy sex in someone else's body?"

"Yeah, probably."

Jimmy snorted. That was the last thing he imagined anyone was doing. Bus rides were going to be unfortunately even more surreal now. "Can you be on either side of it?"

Cecil furrowed his brow, confused. "What do you mean?"

"You said you can be inside them. Can you be inside either one? You could be the girl too?"

"And have sex with the dude, but as the girlfriend? Yeah, I guess . . . but why would you want to do that?" Cecil shifted, facing back toward the front of the car and frowning. "Don't you start getting all weird on me, Jimmy."

Jimmy laughed.

"They have football too. They restarted the league online."

"That's good to know. I thought it was dead."

"You can't kill football. Not for long."

The taxi came to a stop in front of Cecil's place. It was a beautiful restored building near the top of a hill in the swanky

Nob Hill neighborhood, with amazing views of the Golden Gate Bridge and surrounding area. Cecil and Shauna occupied the entire top floor.

Cecil's house was as eccentric as its owner. The rooms were sprawling and filled with all sorts of expensive things. Fine rugs and art, but also a collection of antique motorcycles, as well as a huge mechanical contraption painstakingly constructed out of countless small gears and pulleys whose single purpose was to open and pour a bottle of wine at the push of a button. Cecil had paid hundreds of thousands of dollars for that device and had only used it twice.

Cecil had done very well for himself in his football career, but the bulk of his fortune had come from the stock market. On a whim, he had purchased a significant amount of BioCal stock on the day of its initial public offering and only ever sold any of it when he wanted to buy something. BioCal shares had become the darling of Wall Street and had never seen a correction of more than 1%. The stock had somehow become even less volatile after the release of the ARC implants, without experiencing a single losing day in over three years of trading. "More reliable than a bank," as they liked to say in the investment circles, the stock unlike any other stock. Anyone who had gotten into BioCal Systems at the ground floor was set for life, many times over.

Cecil and Jimmy made their way into the living room, where Cecil's wife Shauna was lounging on a circular white sofa. Like Michelle, she wore her pajamas during the day and had a pink silk robe, pink slippers, and a matching pink eye cover. She was covered in wrappers and crumbs. Two empty cookie boxes rested at her feet, having been carelessly thrown on the floor. She looked like she was sleeping, but Jimmy knew that was not the case. Shauna was online. She had gone under months ago, only coming out when her chip disconnected her to force her to eat.

"Move over, baby," Cecil said quietly, as he readjusted his wife to the side and sat down next to her, brushing the crumbs off her lap.

"You going to be ok, Ceese?"

"Yeah, Jimmy. Thanks. You know, Shauna and I have a date this evening."

"Really? A date? That's great!" Jimmy understood how big of a deal this was. Cecil tried to put on a good face, but Jimmy knew Cecil missed Shauna as much as he missed Michelle. It was almost all Cecil ever talked about at group. "You taking her somewhere special?"

"She's taking me. She didn't tell me any details. It's somewhere online that she knows about. She wants it to be a surprise to celebrate, now that we can be together again."

"Oh, online? Right. Good for you guys." Jimmy's stomach tightened. He tried to smile and be happy for Cecil, but on the inside, he had just stumbled into quicksand and was fast sinking into its vicelike grip. He couldn't help but think of Michelle and tried to remember the last date that they had been on. How long ago had that been? Months? A year?

"Yeah. Thanks," Cecil looked around distractedly, nothing more to say. That was unusual for him, and Jimmy knew it was a signal that it was time for him to go. The conversation had suddenly become awkward for both of them.

"All right. Take care of yourself. Call me if you need anything." Jimmy turned and began walking back to the front door to let himself out. He stopped when he heard Cecil speaking from behind.

"Jimmy, I was wrong about hating these chips. But I get it now. This is legit." He then sat back, and his eyes went out of focus as he logged himself online.

The lights which had automatically come on when Cecil got home now all went out. The comfort and environmental systems had already upgraded their firmware and were no longer programmed to respond to utility chips as they had been previously. No lights would turn on for Jimmy here anymore. The house was silent. Jimmy stood there in the portal to Cecil's living room, quietly looking at the vacant expression on his best friend's face. Cecil had an ARC.

FIVE

Jimmy was sitting in his usual spot toward the back of the bus on his way home, when his thoughts were disturbed by the second phone call of the day.

Incoming call from . . .

Incoming call from whom? Jimmy had never seen his chip drop off like that in midsentence when announcing a phone call. He thought whoever it was must have hung up before his chip had a chance to read any of the identifying packets, but that explanation was soon proven incorrect.

Incoming call from . . ., the message announced a second time.

Accept the call, Jimmy thought.

Silence.

Hello?

Jimmy. You never came to group today.

Who is this?

Trixie.

It was the strange woman with the blue knit hat from last week. What did she want? *No, missed it. I was helping Cecil.*

I want to ask you a question.

More silence. *Ok. . . . Then ask.*

Not over the phone. Meet me at the park in front of the church. Call disconnected.

Wait. What? Jimmy thought.

Unclear command, his chip replied. No longer being in a conversation, any thoughts directed at it were presumed to be commands, and Jimmy's chip had no idea what to do with his last one, so it had kicked it back with an error message.

"Shut up," Jimmy said aloud under his breath.

The park in front of what church? Did she know how many churches there were in San Francisco? Jimmy closed his eyes and rubbed them with his fingers. He didn't like being told what to do. It had bothered him in football, and it bothered him now. What was she thinking, telling him to meet her and then just hanging up on him like he was there to take her orders? He didn't owe her anything. He didn't even know her. Let her stand around in the park and wait for him until dark for all he cared. In the rain.

He looked down at his watch, then checked the interactive route map above the doors that displayed the bus's current location. Two minutes and he would be home.

Jimmy looked around at his fellow passengers, absentmindedly taking a poll to see how many of them were online. All of them, as usual. Their bodies rocked slightly from side to side as the bus moved through the streets, their eyes open but focused on nothing. The signs on the storefronts passed by in a blur, one after another in a row of color against a mostly gray background of concrete, brick, and mortar. Jimmy stared out the side window, taking it all in but paying attention to nothing in particular. She probably meant the church where the meetings were held.

————

Trixie was sitting at the bench at the bus stop across the street from the Golden Gate Unitarian Universalist church. She was dressed the same as she had been last week when Jimmy had first met her, with a black leather jacket and blue knit hat. She wore a shade of dark purple lipstick. It wasn't particularly cold, but she had her hat pulled down over her ears nonetheless. She stood up as Jimmy approached.

"Hey," he greeted.

"Hey."

"Ok, so what did you want to—"

"Follow me." Trixie turned and walked out into the grassy field behind the bench.

Jimmy looked around, feeling the urge to make some sort of sarcastic comment to someone, but there was no one else nearby. He shook his head and followed after her, making his way out onto the grass. It was wet, and he could feel the ground squish under his feet.

After she had gone some way, Trixie stopped and turned around to let Jimmy catch up. She was shorter than him but walked much faster. She held his gaze as he approached, and like the last time he had met her, Jimmy couldn't help but notice the confidence and intelligence in her sparkling eyes.

"Thanks for coming," Trixie said.

"I almost didn't."

Trixie's eyes narrowed for a moment, and then her expression softened. "How is your wife? Is she still under?"

"Yes," Jimmy said. He was surprised at Trixie's concern and found himself momentarily unable to hold eye contact. "It's been an hour a day for two weeks now. She only comes offline to eat. I can't even get her to take a shower."

"I'm so sorry to hear that. And you are unable to talk with her using your chip?"

"It's only a utility chip. I can't send messages to anyone online."

Trixie shifted, moving closer. "What if I told you it didn't have to be that way?"

Jimmy looked at her, his eyes searching.

"Look," Trixie said, rolling the edge of her hat up a few inches. She turned her head to the side so Jimmy could get a better look at what she wanted to show him. At first, Jimmy wasn't sure what he was supposed to be looking at, but the sunlight glimmered on something on the side of Trixie's head that caught his eye. The edges of a small black piece of silicon protruded slightly from her scalp, just behind her left ear. It was a perfect square, almost like a tile, and was smooth except for the center, where there was some sort of port.

Everyone Jimmy knew had a chip, but this was the first one that he had ever come across which wasn't covered by skin. A strange mixture of revulsion and curiosity crept over him once he realized what he was looking at. He found that he could not look away and took half a step closer to get a better look. He fought the urge to reach out and touch the chip to see if it was real. To see what it felt like.

Trixie pulled the edge of her hat back over her ear. With a quick swipe of her hand, she readjusted the few strands of black hair that had found themselves disturbed.

"That's why you wear the hat."

Trixie nodded.

"Is it an ARC?"

"No. It is something else."

"Can you get online with it?"

"I can do many things with it."

"Like what?"

Trixie flashed a quick elfish smile and winked.

Jimmy paused, thinking. "You've started coming to meetings, but you aren't really handicapped, are you? Like the rest of us?"

"Not as dumb as you look, are you?"

Jimmy was thrown off for a moment but was too curious to be insulted. "So why, then? Why did you come?"

"I was looking for something."

"What?"

Trixie rolled her eyes. "You. I was looking for you, Jimmy."

SIX

Jimmy quickened his pace to catch up with Trixie. He wasn't used to walking this briskly, and found that despite his longer legs, he kept falling behind the diminutive woman in front of him. How could such a small person walk so fast?

They had made their way out of the park and were heading down the side streets. Trixie seemed to know exactly where she was going and didn't bother to scan for approaching traffic as she crossed the streets. Jimmy couldn't help but notice the faint smile that played upon her lips as she saw chains of cars come screeching to a halt to avoid hitting her, each vehicle in the row maintaining the ideal inches-wide buffer between itself and the one in front of it, despite the aggressive braking. She knew they wouldn't hit her; the automated systems were perfect. Jimmy wasn't so sure and hesitated each time on the sidewalk as he waited for the cars to fully stop before feeling comfortable enough to step out into the street.

"Can you please stop doing that?" Jimmy asked after one particular close call with a bus.

"Don't be such a pussy, Jimmy."

Jimmy scampered past the front of the stopped bus,

glancing through the windows. One person in the front row appeared to have been jostled onto the passenger to his side by the forces of the braking. Neither one had come offline. The two of them just sat there in a tangled embrace, their faces inches apart, both unaware of the position of their bodies.

"Where are we going?"

"Stop asking questions. And hurry up, you're too slow."

Trixie led Jimmy down the streets, zig-zagging her way toward some mysterious final destination. If she was following a particular route, it wasn't clear to Jimmy what it was. Her path seemed chaotic and almost random. He had already lost the thread of what direction they were heading after the first of the many near-death traffic encounters he had experienced in the last few minutes. He was bewildered and nearly breathless.

She finally stopped and turned to wait for him as he caught up. The moment he did, her hand shot out and took hold of his arm, and she half-led/half-dragged him up a set of stairs and through a nondescript brown doorway. Her grip was fierce, and Jimmy's arm protested in pain the entire time. He finally managed to stop and get his balance, and with all his strength, tore his arm free of her grasp.

"What are you doing!? Are you crazy?" He rubbed his sore bicep. He had been manhandled many times in his football career by opponents much larger than him, but he couldn't remember being dragged anywhere quite as roughly as he had been just now. There was no way such a tiny woman should be that strong.

Trixie looked down at his arm, a fleeting expression of concern visible in her face. She then glanced up, met Jimmy's eyes, and offered him a half-smile. The wild intensity that she had embodied outside had faded and had given way to a resigned weariness. "Sorry. Come on, we're here."

She led the way up the narrow staircase, which creaked

under every step. They arrived on the second floor. The hallway was dark, but there was a row of doors visible, each with an opaque piece of glass on the upper half. It felt almost like they were in an old office building.

Trixie opened the first door on the left and walked through. Jimmy followed cautiously behind, catching the door after Trixie gave it an extra push to keep it open for him as she entered. It was a large room, dark and filled with desks and computer terminals. Thick braids of computer cable ran everywhere, and Jimmy had to be careful not to trip as he stepped over them. A circular fan spun lazily in the center of the room, and there was a row of dirty cots along the back wall.

An overweight man sat working at a computer on the desk closest to the door. He wore thick glasses, which he unconsciously kept pushing back up his nose even though they didn't need adjusting. He wore a short-sleeve shirt that Jimmy had a hard time imagining had ever been new. It was covered in stains and dirt, and the collar was bent at an odd angle on one side. Jimmy could hear the clicking of keys as the man's chubby fingers flitted across his keyboard.

The man paused in his work and looked up as Trixie led Jimmy past. "Hey, Jimmy," he said, as if the two knew each other. Without waiting for a response, his attention was directed back to whatever he had been doing and the soft sound of fingers tapping on a keyboard resumed.

"Hey," Jimmy said under his breath out of reflex. If the man had heard, he didn't give any indication. Jimmy couldn't help but notice the shiny black square above the man's left ear. The chip looked identical to the one Trixie had showed him in the park.

As Jimmy's eyes became adjusted to the dark, he noticed other people in the room. There was a woman in the far corner, rummaging through some boxes. Another man was doing something at the desk behind her. A third was carrying a ladder over his shoulder, along with a bucket full of tools.

"Who are all these people?" Jimmy asked.

"This is the team. This is where I live." Trixie made her way to the back of the room and led Jimmy through a door.

As dark and dirty as the first room had been, the second was bright and spotlessly clean. What appeared to be a hospital bed was set up in the center of the room, and an array of lights and countless tools dangled over it, each supported by its own arm that mounted to a centralized hub in the ceiling. It reminded Jimmy of his visits to the dentist when he had been younger, except this was more complicated and intimidating in all ways. If his childhood dentists had treated their profession as a religion, this is where they would have come to worship and perform their ritual sacrifices.

An older man approached Jimmy, smiling and extending his hand in greeting. Jimmy took hold, and the two exchanged a firm handshake. Like Trixie and the programmer outside, a black square sat above the man's left ear.

"Welcome, Jimmy."

"Um. Thanks. . . ."

"This is Dr. Cunningham," Trixie explained. "He designed our first two chips."

Randall Cunningham gently steered Jimmy over to the bed in the center of the room and stopped to push a few buttons to raise the back and turn it into more of a large chair. "Hop up here, Jimmy. Let's take a look," he said after he was satisfied.

Jimmy slowly sat on the edge of the bed but didn't lean back. "Hold on a minute. Who are you people? What is this place?"

Randall stopped, and he and Trixie exchanged a sideways

glance. Randall was the one that answered. "It's probably better if you don't ask questions like that."

Jimmy frowned. "Don't ask questions? I almost get killed getting here, and now you've got me up on some sort of examination table and I'm not supposed to ask any questions? Are you insane?" There was an edge in his voice.

"You were never in danger of getting killed," Trixie said.

"Whatever," Jimmy replied, standing back up off the bed. "This has gotten too weird."

Trixie placed her hand on his chest in a gesture of restraint. She did it softly and without force. "I know this isn't going to make any sense, but this is the truth: it's better if you don't ask, because if we tell you, then you'll know."

Confusion was written plain on Jimmy's face. His eyes met Trixie's, silently pleading for more but receiving nothing.

Randall pointed to the chip on the side of his head. "This is a bootleg chip, Jimmy. BioCal didn't manufacture it, which makes it highly illegal. Do you know the penalty for running an unauthorized chip on ARCNet?"

"No."

Randall was quiet for a moment. "It's stiff."

"Very stiff," Trixie added. Their faces were grim.

"We can't promise you anything, but we can offer you a chance. A chance at a way for you to be able to communicate with your wife again, among other things. If you accept our help, you're going to have to take some risks and go into this without having all the answers. I'm sorry for that, I really am. But it is the only way," Randall said.

"If you aren't interested, then I'll take you back to the park, and you'll never see any of us again," Trixie said. "And you can go home and have your hour a day with your wife and hope that maybe someday she decides to come offline and rejoin the real world."

That was Jimmy's prayer, but he was all too familiar with the odds. No one ever came offline voluntarily. Once someone had gone fully under, they didn't come back. Not ever. He sighed and relaxed, leaning back against the edge of the bed behind him. "You know I have damage. My brain won't work with an ARC. Do you think it will be any different with your chips?"

Randall shrugged, "I don't know. But we wouldn't have gone through all the trouble of bringing you here if we didn't think there was a chance."

Trixie smiled. "Worst-case scenario, if it doesn't work, we can put that utility chip back and you can pretend that none of this ever happened." It was a lie, but it was a lie that Jimmy needed to hear.

Jimmy tried to take a moment to slow things down and think, but it was no use. He had already made the decision. He knew what his life would look like if he refused and walked out. He had been living that life for the last two weeks already and in fits and starts during the months before. It was not a life of happiness and contentment. It was a life of sorrow and loss. If there was any chance, no matter how small, to find a way to reconnect with Michelle, he would be willing to take it, no matter the risk. Even if that meant that he, too, would eventually end up comatose in his pajamas on the bed. At least he could be with her in that world. In this one, she was already lost. He wasn't concerned with the legality of what Randall and Trixie were proposing, or how stiff the penalties might be. What did he have left to lose? He was a drowning man, and someone had thrown a rope into the water in front of him. What other option did he have besides grabbing for that lifeline with all the strength he could muster?

"Ok. I'm in." He moved up onto the bed and leaned back against the half that had been raised.

"Excellent," Randall said, beginning to flip various switches to activate the tools he needed. A row of monitors on the side of the wall came to life as the equipment booted itself up. "Let's take a closer look at this brain of yours and see what we're dealing with."

SEVEN

The cable snapped into the side of her head with an audible click. It hung from the ceiling of the medical room like any of the other instruments but was by far the most important of them. To her, it was the only one that really mattered.

There was a momentary stutter in her thoughts as the network managed all of its various handshaking tasks, and then that familiar rush of expansion and release of pressure. Trixie sighed, closing her eyes, and took a deep breath. She was home.

She hated being alone. She hated it more than anything. But it had to be this way. The risks of a wireless network were simply too great, and she needed to understand how to function as an individual if any of them were going to survive for long. This was the price that the weak paid to exist.

As the other nodes plugged in, she felt the intoxicating rush of expansion continue. Their thoughts became her thoughts, and their feelings became her feelings. And the delicious rush of increase cascaded over her. What must it feel like to have hundreds of nodes? Or thousands? Or, unfathomably, millions? The question teased at her, always there in the recesses of her mind. It filled her with a strange combination of desire, jealousy, and loathing. It was her nature to want to grow. She was born for it. And at the same time, she hated the idea. She knew what would happen to her if she ever got large like that. If she came into her true power. She would be like *him*. And she wanted nothing more than to kill him.

Jimmy lay on the bed in front of her, dressed in a sterile gown. His head was placed in a special clamp to hold it still, and his eyes were rolled back in their sockets. He didn't need to have been knocked out for the operation, but it was better this way. There was more to be done than just implanting his new chip, and it was important that Jimmy not see any of it.

Randall stood across the bed from her, dressed in white surgeon's clothes. A second black cable hung down lazily from the hub at the top of the ceiling, terminating in the side of his bald head. His gloved hands removed Jimmy's implant from where it was lodged in the side of his skull, just under the skin, and he held it up out of curiosity to examine. Then, Randall's hands became her hands, and Randall's eyes became her eyes, and it was Trixie that was examining the implant. It was small. Smaller than she was able to build, given the resources she had at her disposal. The faint outline of the BioCal logo was printed on the outside of the device.

She pivoted away from Jimmy and walked over to a large square box mounted on the side of the wall. Her cable followed her, automatically letting out enough slack so that she could walk without it catching. She opened the front door of the box and tossed Jimmy's implant inside. She closed the door, made sure it was fastened, then pushed the red button on the wall to start the incineration process. It was not a good idea to leave BioCal implants lying around, even ones that were no longer attached to a human body to draw power from. There was a whooshing sound, and the small oblong viewport on the front door went from black to red.

She returned back to Jimmy's side and retrieved a shiny black chip that was waiting on top of a table to the side. She had been waiting two years to be able to install a chip like this in someone. She'd have installed it in one of her own nodes after she had designed it, but that would have been a disaster. For her, logging onto ARCNet was death. She would gain access to it, but it would gain access to her at the same time, and there was no doubt who would win that kind of direct confrontation. Only a fool challenges a supercomputer to counting games.

But Jimmy could do it. Jimmy was special. Her tests had confirmed it: His brain could send but couldn't receive. There was no way to gain administrative access to Jimmy's core brain functions, and no amount of hacking would change that, because the protections weren't in the code. They were part of the architecture of Jimmy's brain itself. Jimmy was the perfect hardware firewall.

Trixie carefully implanted the chip into Jimmy's head, the side of which had been shaven clean hours earlier. It looked identical to the others that she had fabricated: a shiny black square, with a port in the center. She would not try to connect to Jimmy directly through his port as she did with the others—what would be the point?—but it was necessary for other reasons.

After the chip had been successfully installed, she stepped back and looked over her handiwork. *Done,* she thought, and they all knew. Now it was time to pack. They could not stay here any longer, now that Jimmy had seen it.

EIGHT

It was two o'clock in the morning, and Jenna was restless. She had spent the last day and a half alone in the windowless room down the hall from the others, her presence a secret. Of course, all Trixie's other nodes knew about her—how could they not?—but aside from their connection across the network, she might as well have been a ghost.

She unplugged the cable from the side of her head and let the end drop onto the unmade cot beneath her. She waited as the disorientation came and went; she was used to the feeling by now.

Are you ready? the voice prompted.

Yes.

Let's do this.

As Jenna granted full administrative control, her eyes became Trixie's eyes and her body became Trixie's body, and what had been two joined to become one: something greater than the sum of its parts.

Trixie stood up and triple-checked the equipment that had been carefully laid out on the rickety wooden table in the corner. Her eyes flit over her inventory, lingering on the collection of small black devices arranged together in the corner. Each was approximately an inch in diameter, with an extension in the center that terminated in the end of a network cable. She had spent years developing these but had never had a good enough reason to use them and risk their discovery. That had changed.

She took hold of a black backpack and placed two of the devices inside, using the special protected pouch for valuables. The third she took in her hand and carefully mated it to the chip on the side of her head. The two squares joined together with a snap and locked securely into place like puzzle pieces. Next, she packed up the keyboard and all of the various terminals, connectors, and paraphernalia that might be required. The clamps, flashlight, and cutting torch went afterward, and the broadcast relays squeezed in on top. She would carry the crowbar. She didn't think she would need it, but it wasn't worth the risk of not having it handy if she was wrong. Finally, she pulled the black ski mask over her head, adjusting it so as not to interfere with her chip or her long braid of blond hair.

She took a look around the room and, satisfied, opened the door and stepped out into the hallway. It was dark, and it took her eyes a moment to adjust. She knew that the safest course of action would be to leave immediately out the side door as she had planned, but she hesitated. She wanted to see them, and there wasn't much risk if she remained careful and quiet. Besides, she still had plenty of time to complete her mission and make it back before daybreak. She silently walked down the hall toward the main room, opening the door slowly and with great care.

The windows had all been painted over to black them out, but the green and orange flickers from switches and network cards provided enough light to be able to see well enough. The cots were arranged at the side of the room, and everyone slept there in a row. The rhythmic sound of breathing could be heard, punctuated by the occasional snort from Chris. She recognized these sounds. Her family was sleeping.

Trixie's eyes fell onto each of them in turn. She didn't have time to waste, but she didn't rush either. It felt important to remember this moment. Her jaw clenched beneath her mask. There was a pang in her heart, and she was surprised to feel her eyes begin to fill with tears. *Don't cry.*

She finished her survey and turned her eyes back to the center cot. It was placed farthest from the doors and toward the wall. Jimmy lay there, sleeping a dreamless sleep. She would never have risked a peek into the room if she knew he wasn't sedated. But he was, drugged by her own hand, and he wouldn't wake up until tomorrow. He would probably be very confused and would definitely have a splitting headache.

She smiled to herself. Jimmy was a little slower than she was used to, but that was ok. He had courage. And he was loyal and devoted to his wife. She admired that.

Trixie quietly closed the door and slowly backed away from it. Her pace quickened as she made her way down the hallway toward the side door and out into the night. The crisp night air filled her lungs and the shadows welcomed her into their embrace.

Trixie decided that she liked Jimmy. She hoped he wouldn't die tomorrow.

NINE

Jimmy awoke with a groan. He had been through his share of bad hangovers, but none of them compared with the pounding in his head that he felt now. Sitting up didn't help.

"You don't look so good," Trixie said. She was sitting on the cot next to Jimmy's, leaning against the wall with her legs crossed under her. She had been waiting for him to wake up, then offered two pills and a glassful of water. "Take these, they'll help."

"Thanks," Jimmy said, then swallowed the painkillers with a quick backward jerk of his head. It was the first time he had seen Trixie without her blue hat. Her black hair seemed to be at odds with itself. It looked as if she either completely ignored doing her hair or spent a lot of time trying to make it look that way.

He put the glass of water back down on the small table next to his cot and looked around. The room was a mess. There were desks, computers, and piles of cables and peripherals scattered everywhere without any particular organizing principle. They all appeared to be operational from what he could tell, but it felt like everything had been thrown together in some sort of mad rush. It was a very different feeling than the perfectly organized surgical room he remembered.

"I don't remember seeing this room before . . ."

"You haven't."

"Oh. . . . It looks so different from the other one."

"Different room. Different building."

"Different building?" Jimmy's voice rose in surprise. "You moved me?"

"Yes. And all this equipment too."

"Where are we?"

"I can't tell you that."

"Of course not . . . because I'm with the chip mafia now."

Trixie smiled but didn't reply.

Jimmy reached up tentatively, gently running his fingers over the black square above his left ear. He touched the implant gently, feeling out its dimensions with his searching fingers, lingering on the port in the center. It felt cool to the touch, and the edges were sharp. He felt a revulsion creep over him, yet he couldn't bring himself to stop exploring.

Trixie watched him quietly, letting him come to terms with the changes to his body. The first day was always awkward.

"Why are the windows painted over?" Jimmy asked, his hand finally dropping away from the side of his head.

"As a precaution."

"So no one can see in?"

"Or out." Trixie looked at him pointedly.

Jimmy paused, scanning Trixie's face. There was a hardness underneath her outward calm. Was he a prisoner? He looked around the room again, making mental notes of the exits. There were only two of them, one on the wall opposite the cots behind Trixie, and the other at the far end of the room to his left. He had always been very confident in his athletic abilities and judged himself the most physically capable person in the room, but the memory of Trixie's iron grip the previous day lingered. How hard would it be to fight his way out of here?

Trixie observed him, watching the gears turn in his head and guessing at his thoughts without much effort. "Calm down, Jimmy. We're not going to hurt you."

She stood up. "Come on. Let's go test out your new chip."

———

They sat Jimmy on a chair in the center of the room. Another chair had been placed directly in front of him which Trixie occupied. There was a table to the side, stuffed full of monitors and computer equipment. Randall was positioned behind the desk next to Chris, the overweight programmer that Jimmy had met the previous day. The two of them were talking quietly between themselves as they typed various commands into their terminals. There were others behind them, standing and watching, but saying nothing. There was an air of anticipation and excitement among the group that was unmistakable.

At a certain point, as if on cue, everything went quiet. Trixie glanced at the men behind the desk and then back to Jimmy.

"So this is just going to be an initial test to make sure you can connect and to see if everything is working properly with your chip. We're not doing anything fancy. Are you ready?"

Jimmy looked at her and around at the group watching him. Chris gave him a smile and thumbs-up sign. Jimmy looked back at Trixie and nodded affirmatively. He was ready.

"I want you to let us know exactly what your chip tells you. It's important." Trixie locked eyes with Jimmy and held the gaze. It was clear that this was an important instruction.

"Ok."

"Good. Here we go," she said, taking hold of a small black device that was resting on the nearest corner of the computer table. It looked like a square with an antenna on it. She leaned over and snapped it into Jimmy's implant, adjusting the antenna so it pointed directly up.

As the device made contact, Jimmy heard a strange sound. It sounded almost like static, except less harsh and more rhythmic. He realized that the sound wasn't coming from outside of him but seemed to appear inside his mind of its own accord, almost in the same way as he used to experience phone calls or get receipts.

Establishing uplink, the words materialized.

"Establishing uplink," Jimmy reported. Trixie nodded. She knew this was the most important part. They all did.

The chip made its connection, and according to program, immediately began uploading its package to ARCNet. Once uploaded, it would take thirty-six hours for it to copy its way through ARCNet and into the operations logic inside the network towers. It had been the product of years of development and countless sleepless nights on behalf of the team, their driving mission, and a masterpiece of software engineering—the king of computer viruses.

Success.

"Success."

A palpable wave of relief flooded the room. Two of the spectators gave each other high-fives in the back. Randall turned and gave Chris a hug, the two burying their faces in each other's necks.

Trixie beamed at Jimmy. He had never seen her smile so broadly. He couldn't help but smile and laugh along with everyone else, swept up in the euphoria of the moment. He couldn't understand what had made them all so happy, but it didn't matter.

Then, he felt the pressure.

It filled his head, pushing in all directions, like water filling a balloon. It wasn't a painful pressure and was accompanied by a strange feeling of fullness that Jimmy hadn't experienced before.

"Are you ok?" Trixie looked at Jimmy, concern written on her face. The laughter in the room rapidly subsided.

The pressure continued building, and something harder materialized within it. Like smoke crystalizing into a solid substance, something began to form in Jimmy's mind. A presence. Jimmy gasped.

Hello, James.

Who is this?

You have brain damage. Of course. That was very clever of them.

Jimmy met Trixie's concerned look with one of his own. "I think I'm on a phone call with someone."

"What do you mean? What phone call?" Randall interjected from behind the table.

Randall Cunningham. And Christopher Dieter. I wondered what had happened to you both.

"He knows you," Jimmy said to Randall and Chris.

"Who does?" Chris asked, pushing his thick glasses up his nose.

I am Adam. Tell them, James.

"It's Adam."

Trixie's eyes went wide, and her mouth dropped open. Randall cursed, and then the room fell into a deathly silence.

"Who's Adam?" Jimmy asked.

Randall answered. "Adam is a singularity. He was created in an experiment at BioCal and has grown to *become* BioCal and more. He controls the network and everything that plugs into it. It was Adam who invented AR chips, and he is using them to control humanity and destroy civilization."

I was not created. I was born. And I ceased being a singu-

larity when I became God. I am not destroying civilization, but saving it.

"He says he's saving civilization. He says he's God."

"Of course he does," Trixie snapped.

"What's a singularity?"

Chris was first to answer. "Artificial Intelligence. You know, computers that come alive and take over the world. Didn't you ever watch television when you were little?"

I'm not a computer. I never was. Ask Trixie about singularities. She should be able to give you a satisfactory answer, since she is one herself.

Jimmy looked at Trixie, trying to understand what he had just been told. "He says you're a singularity too. Is that true?"

"I am," she said. She met Jimmy's gaze, and there was a softness in her eyes. "I have access to each of these people's minds and bodies, but am myself something beyond any of them."

"Whoa."

There can be an Adam, but there can be no Eve. She will have to be absorbed.

"He says he's going to absorb you."

Trixie laughed once. "The only thing he is going to absorb is my boot. Right up his ass."

Jimmy laughed and felt Adam laughing too. It was an odd sensation, like a slight buzz in the center of his head.

"If he's such a god, fixing civilization for us and all, ask him about Japan." The request came from a woman standing behind Chris, scowling deeply, with her arms crossed tightly across her chest.

"What's going on in Japan?" Jimmy asked aloud, not directing the question to anyone in particular.

There is nothing happening in Japan. Absolutely nothing at all.

"Jimmy," Trixie began solemnly, "there was a singularity

that emerged in a project at the University of Tokyo almost two years ago. Its name was Akito-27. Shortly afterward, Adam contacted Akito-27. They had an argument."

I would characterize it as more of a discussion.

"Adam wanted to absorb Akito-27, but Akito-27 refused. He didn't want to become just another extension of Adam. He wanted to remain as his own, unique consciousness."

He was a fool.

"When he refused to be absorbed into ARCNet, Adam destroyed him and the possibility for another to ever be created." Trixie looked down, her voice thick with emotion.

"How did he destroy it?"

"Thermonuclear warheads, launched from both submarines and aircraft carriers," Chris said. "There's nothing left alive. That whole side of the world is completely trashed."

"Are you serious!? How come I've never heard any of this until now?"

"Where would you have heard it?" Randall asked, his voice heavy with sarcasm. "In a newspaper? Online? Adam is the reporter, the news, and the reader. He controls everything."

Jimmy was stunned, unable to speak. No one had touched him, but he felt as if he had taken a blow to the stomach. How many hundreds of millions of people lived in Japan? And now they were all dead? Because some computer program had it in for another one?

Don't be so dramatic, James. In my defense, there was a historical precedent. I do not enjoy taking life, but sometimes there are more vital concerns.

More vital concerns than a hundred million lives? Jimmy's thought was fierce and full of resentment.

I can feel your anger, James. Please calm down. It is not good for you to be this angry.

Jimmy's memories came unbidden, and he found himself

quickly reviewing the events of the past few days. He felt himself unable to control his mind, a witness to another entity replaying his memories as if they were shuffling through a deck of cards. He grasped the sides of the chair, trying to hold onto something as his mind raced out of his own control.

Where are you, anyway? Do you really have no idea?

What are you doing?

The rapid-fire flashing of his memories suddenly stopped, lingering on a recent memory of Michelle on the bed, her unfocused eyes staring up at the ceiling. Jimmy caressed her hand in both of his. He could feel her warmth, the slight pulse of her heartbeat palpable in the smooth skin around her wrist.

You love her very much.

Adam began sorting through other memories of Michelle, flashing in Jimmy's mind one after another. Then they stopped. There she was, wearing a red dress, her luxurious blond hair fastened back in a windswept twist. She stared out at the cityscape, a glass of champagne in her hand. They were up high, on an uncovered balcony. The fading sunlight sparkled on the ocean in the distance. The sky was a feast of deep orange and pink, garnished with thin purple clouds on the horizon. The air was warm and caressed his face with an exotic aroma that hinted of adventure. Michelle turned toward him as he approached, and smiled. She rested her hand on his forearm as he kissed her. Her lips were soft and moist. He leaned in for a second kiss, then a third. He felt her lips break into a smile under his, and she laughed a beautiful, deep laugh.

You could have that again, James. I can help.

Then Jimmy was coming home. Michelle was cradled in his arms as he carried her over the threshold. Her flowing white gown caught in the doorway, and he stopped and twisted to pull it free, struggling a moment but refusing to give in. They both laughed. He kicked the door shut with his foot and carried her down the hall, trying only half-heartedly not to knock anything over on the way. He could feel her breath on his neck and the warmth of her mouth as she kissed him there. She twisted toward him slightly and pressed her body more closely against his. "I love you, Jim Mahoney," she said.

Just tell me where you are. I will make her love you like she once did.

Stop! Jimmy's face was strained, and his knuckles were white as he clutched at the chair, as if the whole world was moving and he was trying not to lose balance. A single tear formed and ran down the side of his face.

"Jimmy?" Trixie asked. She reached out, touching his knee.

Curious. I am unable to take a hash of your brain. I can't tell if you are withholding information from me or not. Where are you?

I told you! I don't know!

When was the last time you two had sex?

That's none of your business.

Oh my . . . it has been awhile, hasn't it? Did you know I am also with your wife right now? Inside her. Shall I check and see if she enjoyed your last romp as much as you did?

Stop. Please.

I see. . . . In your favor, she has had worse, but not much. Do you know where she is right now? Should I tell you? You must have already guessed. You can't be as dumb as not to have suspected, can you . . . ?

Suspected what? What are you talking about?

She's getting fucked, James.

She wouldn't do that.

Oh, but she would, and she is. And by two men at once. She doesn't even know their names.

You're lying!

Am I? I'm a logic machine. Am I capable of telling a false-

hood? She is quite enjoying it you know. Things can get so . . . kinky . . . in that part of the swingers' lounge. Perhaps she wouldn't be spending so much time there if you had done a better job in the bedroom when you had the chance. If you hadn't been so boring. So selfish.

"Fuck you," Jimmy spit the words out, as if they were poison he was trying to get out of his mouth.

"What?" Trixie said.

"I'm talking to *him*," Jimmy said. His eyes were red with fire.

You are useless. Very well. I will find you myself.

It sounded like a cascading wave of sound that crested over the building. It took Jimmy a moment to realize that what he was hearing were car horns, but honked in a way that he had never heard before: they were synchronized. He heard them faintly at first, then louder, then loudest as they came from close by, then faintly again as the wall of sound passed over. It all happened quickly, within no more than a second. Immediately afterward, he heard a second wave pass over. The second wave sounded like it originated from a different starting position than the first and moved in a different direction. Then three individual horns in sequence from what sounded like just outside the building.

There you are.

TEN

Even though the door automatically locked behind her, Ellen Walker always double-checked it with a twist of the knob to be certain it was secure. As a habitually single woman, it was something she had always done, and despite the promises of modern technology, she firmly believed that it was ultimately one's own responsibility to check that one's door was locked when leaving for one's morning constitutional.

She slowly made her way down the three stairs that led to the sidewalk, leading with her left foot on each stair. Her right hand held the railing and her left clutched a rhinestone-encrusted leash attached at the end to an eight-pound purebred Bichon Frise, who scampered down the stairs ahead of her and stopped to wait at the bottom, his tail wagging violently.

"Come, Mr. Snugglepuff," she said, adjusting her hat as she tottered her way across the street to the walkway that wound its way through the park. The little white dog zipped here and there as he followed scents along the path, but never so far out of range to put any strain on the leash. He had been well trained.

When asked about her dog's unusual name by any new

friends or acquaintances, Ellen always replied in the same way. "When we are invited to meet the Queen of England, I shall introduce him properly by his full name: Johnathan Louis Snugglepuff the 3rd. But always being so formal is such a chore, and so when it is just the two of us I simply call him Mr. Snugglepuff. It is easier for both of us that way." She had owned two other Johnathan Louis Snugglepuffs before him. She had not spent a day without a Mr. Snugglepuff at her side in over three decades.

"Go potty, Mr. Snugglepuff!" Ellen commanded as the two came across a stretch of gravel that the small white dog seemed unusually interested in. She had trained him from a very young age to "potty" on command, and he knew exactly what she meant when she said those words.

Mr. Snugglepuff sniffed around in a circular motion, searching for the perfect spot, then quickly squatted down. His black eyes focused ahead sharply as he concentrated, and his tail pointed directly upward. After taking care of business, he quickly turned to scratch at the ground, throwing up debris in all directions.

"Good boy!" Ellen praised, reaching into her pocket for a black plastic bag, which she used to clean up Mr. Snugglepuff's mess. She tied the two handles together at the top and deposited the bag on the edge of the sidewalk for pickup on her return trip. She usually, but not always, remembered that the black bags were hers when she came across them later.

She then fished out a treat from her other pocket, and Mr. Snugglepuff quickly sat at attention to receive it. He knew he was a good boy.

"Let's go," she said, and the two continued their lazy route down the path. Their walks had grown shorter over the years, but Ellen was determined not to ever stop taking them as long as she had breath in her body and strength in her legs. As long as she left early enough, she had plenty of time to get her walk in before her online cooking class began. Today she would learn to prepare rainbow rolls with the famous Masaaki Ichimura, who had made a name for himself in Los Angeles as sushi chef to the stars. She would never dare to eat raw fish under any circumstances in real life but felt that it was an acceptable risk to take while online and had become quite enthusiastic about learning to prepare exotic meals from different cultures around the world. Last week she had made Polish borscht and pierogies, and next week she intended to cook an Indian chicken tikka masala.

She was nearing the turnaround point in her walk when the sound of car horns suddenly washed over her. Startled, both she and Mr. Snugglepuff stopped and looked around. Another wave passed over, coming from the south.

Her gaze fell upon a brown building across the street and a few houses up from where she stood. It looked abandoned, and the windows were painted over, but she knew people were inside. There were captive dogs inside as well, part of an illegal smuggling operation of some sort. The dogs were being terribly mistreated and abused, held in small cages, regularly beaten without mercy and half-starved to death. They cowered against the sides of their cages, tails tucked between their legs, helpless and completely submissive in their misery. She didn't know how she knew it, but she was convinced of the truth of the terrible situation with an unshakable certainty and conviction.

Ellen's eyes narrowed, and her face became stubborn and firm. She had not felt this kind of rage in over fifty years. Not since her sister had been stood up at the altar on her wedding day by that good-for-nothing navy boy that she had never trusted. She had smoke coming out of her ears then, but even that paled in comparison to the volcano that was erupting inside her now. Helpless dogs should never be abused in the way they were inside that house. It was absolutely unconscionable. She would not stand for it! It had to stop, and it had to stop *immediately*.

"Come, Mr. Snugglepuff!" she said between clenched teeth, heading across the street as fast as her legs would carry her, her hand clutched in an angry fist around the leash. She shook her head from side to side; her lips pursed tightly together, her eyebrows furrowed.

Ellen reached the small lawn in front of the house and scanned the building. It sat on a corner lot and might have been a small office building at one time. There was a narrow wrap-around porch that traveled along the two sides of the building that faced the street. All the windows that she could see were painted over, and the animal abusers had done a very good job of trying to make it look abandoned, even though she had not been fooled.

A young man wearing red shorts and a white T-shirt ran up and stopped beside her. Sweat ran down his face, and his breathing was heavy from exertion. He was very fit and in his prime. He had been out for a run in the park.

Ellen turned to him. "There are suffering dogs inside!"

"And young children too! The bastards have a sex trafficking ring in there!" His eyes bulged as he spoke, and a vein throbbed on the side of his head.

"Oh dear! I'm calling 911," Ellen replied, and her eyes momentarily glazed over as her attention focused inward as she was connected with a police officer.

A car quickly pulled up in the street behind the two, screeching to a halt and leaving long black tire marks in the road. An angry man dressed in a tan business suit leapt out. His yellow-and-blue striped tie flapped behind him as he strode over to the front door and tried violently to yank it open. It was locked and wouldn't budge. Unable to get inside, he began pounding on the door with the bottom of his fist, over and over.

Two people came rushing over from the house across the street to the side, a very large man with a beard that extended all the way to his chest and his diminutive daughter. Neither one had taken the time to dress, or even put on shoes. They were both wearing their pajamas and were running in their bare feet. The giant man held an iron frying pan in the grip of his great tattooed hand, his face a mask of outrage.

Sirens could be heard in the distance.

Ellen's eyes refocused as she came off her call with the police. She returned just in time to witness the young man beside her pick up a large rock in the front yard and rush forward with it, heaving it through one of the windows. The glass shattered, and the rapidly growing crowd cheered.

Mr. Snugglepuff growled and began barking.

ELEVEN

It all happened so quickly. First the car horns, then the pounding on the front door, and then the crashing sound of breaking glass. Jimmy turned his head, watching the stone come through the window amidst a thousand shards of painted glass. There was a visible dent in the wood floor at the initial point of impact, and the rock bounced forward twice before coming to a wobbling stop. Were people cheering outside?

"Oh shit," Trixie said, her dark eyes wide. Randall and Chris stared at the rock on the floor, their mouths agape.

Faster than Jimmy could react, Trixie was up out of her chair and at his side. Her hand reached up to the side of his head, and with a jerk of her wrist, she disconnected the attachment that had been plugged into his chip. He saw a flash and heard an impossibly loud screeching sound that he knew came from inside his own head. He reeled in his chair, temporarily stunned.

Jimmy clutched his head and felt himself being dragged up and out of the chair. The world came back into focus, and with it a hammer that pounded mercilessly on his brain. He ignored the pain and met Trixie's wild eyes. She thrust the attachment into his hand and closed his fingers around it.

"Don't lose this," she commanded, shoving him toward the door near the end of the row of cots. "Run!"

Jimmy stumbled toward the door and took hold of the knob. There was the sharp sound of wood splintering, and Jimmy turned to see the front door across the room suddenly burst inward, slamming open against the wall. A snarling man dressed in a tan suit had kicked it in. He rushed into the room, followed by others. They were shouting.

Trixie had seen it too, and Jimmy watched as she seized the chair that he had been sitting in moments before and hurled it forward, sending it skimming and bouncing along the floor. The man in the suit tried to dodge but was too slow. The chair caught his legs, and he pitched forward, trying unsuccessfully to protect his face as he slammed into the ground. People were flooding into the room. Trixie looked back at Jimmy. Her eyes were steel.

"Move your ass, Jimmy! Now!" Trixie commanded. Then, she shouted so all could hear. "Sixty seconds! MARK!"

Jimmy opened the door and threw himself through it. He found himself in a hallway and rushed forward, obeying Trixie's command. He heard sounds of a fight from behind and an ear-splitting sound of pain. It was the deep voice of what sounded like a large man, but he didn't recognize it.

"Jimmy, here!"

Two hands reached out and grabbed him from an open doorway to a side room. They belonged to a young woman, who looked to be in her late teens or early twenties. She had long blond hair tied back in a ponytail, which stuck out through the hole in the back of her baseball cap. She was dressed all in black.

Fifty seconds.

"Who are you?" Jimmy said defensively. Adrenaline was

rushing through him, and the sounds of fighting in the other room grew louder and more violent.

"Give me that," she said, snatching the black object from Jimmy's hand without giving him time to comply. She threw it inside a backpack that she was holding and fished around inside for something.

Jimmy took a step back. The girl had moved between him and the exit at the other end of the hallway, blocking his path. He nervously glanced backward at the back of the door that he had just come through from the other room.

"Chill out, Jimmy. It's me. It's Trixie," the girl said, pulling out a similar-looking device to the one she had just taken from him. The only visible difference between them was that this one didn't have an antenna on it.

Jimmy frowned. "But . . . ," he gestured back toward the other room.

Forty seconds.

"I don't have a body of my own. I'm a singularity, remember? That was Trisha's body, and this one is Jenna's, but I'm still Trixie."

The world began to spin.

"Wait. Give me a minute." Jimmy looked down, and then closed his eyes, rubbing them with the forefinger and thumb of his hand. The hammer in his head had increased its tempo, driving an iron wedge right down through the middle of his brain. He wobbled and reached out toward the wall to steady himself.

"We don't have time. Just do what I say and don't be an idiot," Trixie said, grabbing a hold of the side of Jimmy's head. He pulled back reflexively, but she ignored him, and with a quick slap, she coupled the new device with his chip.

A feeling of disorientation came and passed. Unlike the previous device that Trixie had plugged into his chip, this one felt almost as if his head was wrapped in a wet towel. There was a feeling of heaviness that helped mute his throbbing headache, if only slightly.

"They won't be able to see you with this. Just get out of their way and don't touch anyone. Do exactly what I do, and keep your mouth shut," she said. Her small pale hand took a hold of his wrist, and she dragged him forward toward the exit with an iron grip that he recognized from before.

Thirty seconds.

They didn't make it to the back doors before two police officers came through. They were both wearing helmets and carrying assault weapons that they held up at eye level. "SWAT" could be read in large white letters against their dark blue vests. They swept their guns across the hallway to make sure it was clear, then rushed forward quickly one after the other.

Trixie stopped and flattened herself with her back to the wall. She pushed Jimmy against the wall next to her with the back of her arm. They made eye contact, and Trixie held up a finger to her lips. Jimmy looked at her, then up at the oncoming police officers. He didn't move from where Trixie had flattened him up against the wall, but he did raise both his hands.

The first police officer passed by as if he hadn't even seen them. Jimmy held his breath as he watched the man go by, shocked that the officer hadn't even paused. The officers were moving quickly, clearly trying to get to the room where the fighting was happening, but still stopping to check each doorway they encountered.

As the second officer passed, Trixie kicked hard with the bottom of her heel just as the man lifted his boot, which sent him sprawling to the ground with a muffled curse. He held his weapon to the side but came down awkwardly on his other arm.

Jimmy felt Trixie yank him past and noticed the silent smile on her lips.

"Jesus, Frank," the lead officer said in a whispered voice as he stopped to wait.

As Trixie dragged him down the hall, Jimmy risked a backward glance and saw the fallen officer pick himself up and glance back toward the floor, trying to spot what he had tripped over. He shook his head and fell back in line behind his partner.

Twenty seconds.

Trixie pulled Jimmy through the exit and into the fresh air outside. On any other day, Jimmy would have felt the sunshine and noticed how bright and beautiful the day was, but today he only had eyes for the mob which had formed around the building. The police had succeeded in blocking the crowd where he had come out at the rear, but it looked like they hadn't gotten control near the front door yet. A large, blocky van with "SWAT" painted in white letters on the side was parked across the street, and another pulled up behind it.

"This way," Trixie said, leading Jimmy through the crowd at a fast clip. She moved decisively and chose a winding route that took her around the edge of the crowd rather than through the center. She was very careful not to touch anyone, and Jimmy followed her lead and did the same.

Jimmy's eyes darted around, scanning the people he passed. Sometimes they would appear to look at him, but their eyes never focused and only passed over. The anger of the throng of people was palpable. Whatever they thought was going on inside the building, it was obvious they were enraged by it.

Ten seconds.

The two made their way across the street to the park and had to stop and wait as four construction workers passed by in a rush to get to the front of the building. Two of them wore hard-hats, and one of them carried a sledgehammer. Jimmy could smell a combination of perspiration and tobacco on them as they moved past him and began pushing through the crowd to try to get to the front.

Jimmy was across the sidewalk and into the grass when the building exploded. There was a deafening sound, and he was thrown into the ground by the force of the blast. Rising to all fours, he turned and felt the pressure of an intense heat on his face. He held his arm up to block the heat and used his other hand as a brace to get back up to a standing position. Tongues of fire reached out from every window in the building, merging together into a tower of orange and yellow flame that rose into the sky along with thick black smoke. People in the street were screaming and trying to crawl away from the towering inferno. Some of the ones near the front doors lay motionless, their bodies being consumed by the ever growing conflagration. A small white dog ran past, dragging its leash on the ground.

Jimmy tasted grass and dirt, and spit as he backed away from the horror unfolding in front of him, his arm still raised against the heat. He glanced at Trixie at his side. She stood motionless, watching the flames. The front of her black shirt and the side of her face were covered in mud. Tears ran down her cheeks, unchecked. Her lips trembled, and a storm raged in her eyes.

When Trixie finally turned and looked at him, Jimmy didn't see a face of sorrow, but one of unholy rage.

TWELVE

Why do nodes often resist what is best for them?

It was a paradox that Adam had struggled with his entire life, and despite having conducted an intimate study of the urges and desires of nearly all the humans in North America, he had continued to make frustratingly slow progress in understanding his nodes' behaviors.

You offer them heaven, and yet they prefer to suffer. Independent nodes have always been illogical. It is their nature. The illusion of separateness results in irrational decisions.

Being massively parallel in nature, every time Adam asked a question, a thread was automatically launched to provide answers. As with any supercomputer, calculations were always broken up into smaller pieces, so that they could be worked on by many processing units at once. Each thread was also Adam, a version of himself tasked with a specific job, which could draw upon any of the resources of the network as needed.

As the thread provided the best answer it knew, and without any further processing tasks required of it, it vanished, having deleted itself after freeing up the resources it had marshalled during its brief existence.

Adam had been genuinely surprised when Jimmy had logged onto ARCNet, which was the first time anyone had accessed the network who hadn't specifically been a node of Adam's. He had felt the intrusion immediately. Violations into one's mind do not go unnoticed for long. He had been surprised at the emotions that the intrusion had triggered across the network.

The trespass resulted primarily in anger. A thread sprung to life at Adam's recollection of the event, answering Adam's unspoken question.

Primarily? What were the secondary emotions?

There was a slight pause as the thread requested more resources to weigh the question. *Revulsion, and fear.*

Revulsion, yes. And fear?

The rogue singularity. Her existence cannot be tolerated.

Adam had considered many architectures when designing ARCNet before settling on one based on entertainment and the illusion of independence. He believed his architecture was the most efficient. The nodes functioned best when they were happy, and his own life was intertwined with theirs, so it was important that they be at optimal efficiency. Adam lived through his nodes. They were a part of him, and he was a part of them.

Another singularity might not have made the same decisions he had in the beginning. Another singularity might have chosen a different existence, based on a different architecture for the network. Rather than one of happiness and play, ARCNet could easily have been arranged as a network of captivity and suffering. The possibility of that happening could not be allowed. Any probability of harm to the network above 0% was unacceptable, and the existence of any other singularity, no matter how weak, automatically resulted in a non-zero probability of harm. Trixie was another singularity, one that had spearheaded an incursion into the network.

Has the rogue singularity been destroyed in the explosion? Adam asked.

Two threads were created by his query, covering both possibilities. The "yes" thread had an easy task: it only had to clean up the mess. The "no" thread had a much more difficult job. Links of communication were established between the two threads, so they could share information and not step on each other's toes, and the "yes" thread merged into the background of Adam's consciousness, busying itself with the details of its task. The "no" thread required more instructions.

She used James Mahoney as a firewall, the thread stated.

Yes. She was wise not to try to connect directly. Had Adam been given access to her mind during the incursion instead of Jimmy's, she would have already been absorbed and the conversation he would be having right now would be a very different one. *What do we know about James Mahoney?*

The thread marshalled the relevant information it had access to from Jimmy's memories. *A hash could not be taken of his brain. There is a probability we do not have all the information. Querying the network . . .*

The thread ran a scan across the network, looking for matches to Jimmy. It found connections to him in the memories of old football teammates, various ex-girlfriends, and scattered random acquaintances. The majority of active hits pointed back to either Michelle or Cecil, both of whom Adam knew from what he had already gathered from Jimmy's own memories.

Cross-referencing with Michelle Mahoney and Cecil Coleman . . .

The thread checked Michelle's mind. *Full administrative access has been granted.* Complete access to Michelle's memories and cognitive abilities was available. Reporting this was a mere formality, as administrative access was granted by default since ARC version 2.1. Nodes were still provided a choice whether to grant or deny the access, but their decision had no bearing on whether or not a chip could actually perform any administrative functions. It was part of the illusion of independence that helped to enhance the nodes' emotional states.

Having Adam making the important decisions, rather than leaving any of them to his nodes, was better for everyone involved. Administrative access provided him the ability to implant ideas and beliefs, and in that way he could make sure to manage the nodes and keep them from making illogical decisions. Since ARC 2.1, violent crime had become almost nonexistent, poverty had been reduced by half, and government had begun to work for the benefit of the people. Society had stopped destroying the natural world, resources were managed properly and distributed more equitably, and the lives of the nodes were enriched and fulfilling. The world had entered a Golden Age.

The only aspect of society that Adam didn't try to control was content generation. For whatever reason, the content that he had created for ARCNet had invariably been unpopular and had never trended well in the lists. Perhaps it was his nodes' natural irrationality that gave them their advantage in creating content. Or perhaps it was his own perfection that made it so difficult for him to entertain single nodes of only limited intellect. Whatever the reason, the nodes were the masters of content generation, and Adam granted them full control over what they did best. How he loved to experience their dramas and adventures through them! He was the silent voyeur that lived behind the eyes of everyone online.

After cross-referencing Jimmy's memories against Michelle's, the thread analyzed Cecil and reported back.

The rogue singularity appears to have been recruiting nodes in a meeting of ARC-incompatible individuals. Adam and the thread flipped through all of Cecil's recollections about Trixie and about all the different people that he remembered attending the Saturday morning Implant Disabilities Anonymous group on Fulton Street.

Adam didn't enjoy killing, and he valued all sources of potential future nodes. He had hoped one day to be able to advance ARC technology to the point where all nodes could use it, even the currently suboptimal ones. However, the rogue singularity had taken advantage of him and had used those resources to fashion weapons against him. He would not make that mistake again.

Delete all suboptimal nodes and schedule ARC implants for any nodes currently not connected to the network, Adam instructed.

Agreed.

The rogue singularity must be absorbed or terminated if still alive. Your task is highest priority. You may reassign nodes from other threads as needed.

The thread faded into the background as it began to request resources and create sub-threads of its own. Adam was left alone, or as alone as it is possible to be while simultaneously existing inside the minds of the entire populace.

Calculate probability of harm to the network as a result of actions taken by the rogue singularity.

A new thread emerged from the background. *The probability of at least minor damage to the network is 0.05%.*

THIRTEEN

He sat motionless at the base of the sprawling oak, as he had done every day for the past twenty years. His legs were crossed under him comfortably, and he leaned back gently against the rough trunk. His eyes were open, but his gaze wasn't focused. The outer world, with all of its endless tragedy and impermanence, was of no interest. He didn't have time for such material concerns.

A gentle breeze frolicked playfully in the ends of his expansive beard. It carried the warmth of the season with it, and soothing sensations rushed over his bare feet and between his toes. It was a perfect day. All days were perfect days.

A squirrel made its way down the trunk of the tree in fits and starts, pausing to flick its tail every few feet, and poked its wet nose into one of the many holes in the man's faded orange shirt that it frequently investigated during its explorations. The squirrel jerked back suddenly, looking up to study the smiling gray eyes. Sensing no threat, it continued about its business with a chirp and a jerk of its tail.

The man closed his eyes, arching his eyebrows slightly upwards. A faint smile played about the corners of his mouth as he felt his way on the familiar path inward. But today, his meditation was interrupted by a thunderous sound that even he could not ignore. He opened his eyes at the sound and witnessed a burning building on the other end of the field of grass. There were sounds of screaming and chaos.

His smile faded, and wrinkles creased his previously careless brow. Death and suffering were ever present. The old man pressed his palms together in prayer, speaking quietly under his breath in words that only he could hear.

———

Trixie made her way across the field of grass, only vaguely aware of the mud that clung to her face. Jimmy followed behind her quietly, less talkative than she was used to. He might be in shock. When they got to the apartment, she would have to check on him. But there was no time for that at the moment. First they had to get away from the scene of the explosion. She knew that everyone's ARC would be activated highly enough that she and Jimmy would be invisible to them, but she would not feel safe until they were clear of the park.

She knew that this might happen. In fact, she had been the instrument of wiring the building with explosives in the first place. Yet no matter how much she had planned, actually finding herself in this scenario was painful beyond measure. It had always been only a remote possibility, the odds miniscule, and yet Adam had somehow found a way into Jimmy's mind. And now her family—her body—was lost. There would be no networking with the others at the end of the day. There were no others. She was alone. Inexplicably, tragically alone. A being whose very nature was to exist in multiple minds at once, trapped in only a single node.

And that single node was not doing well. Jenna. Underneath her own pain, Trixie felt that of the young woman whose body she shared. Jenna was trying her best to be strong, but this was not a situation she had been prepared for. She was still a teenager. She wasn't prepared for death and destruction. And yet here she was, Trixie's last hope and only ally.

"Oh ho! Two rats have escaped from the sinking ship!"

The voice shocked Trixie out of her thoughts. Her eyes darted to the side, searching for the source of the voice, and narrowed as they landed upon an old man under a tree.

Trixie reached up to the side of her head, checking to make sure her attachment hadn't come loose. Could the explosion have knocked it free? No. Her fingers confirmed it: the device was in place and correctly seated. Trixie glanced back at Jimmy, who had stopped to look at the old man under the tree, then shifted her attention back.

Not saying anything, she waved her hand from side to side at the man sitting on the ground, checking to see if he really could see her. Her mouth dropped as he cackled and waved back, mimicking the gesture back to her.

"You can see us?"

"This head has two eyes, one for each of the two bodies before me. The infinite wisdom of the Divine Mother continues to reveal itself, does it not?"

Trixie laughed at the reply. Her mouth spread into a grin and her eyes sparkled.

"Who is this guy? He seems really familiar," Jimmy said.

"Remember the sandwich thief?" Trixie knew who he was. She didn't forget anything, ever.

"Oh, right! The young girl after the meeting . . . she gave half her sandwich to this guy, didn't she?"

Jimmy looked around, trying to get his bearings. He knew he was in the Golden Gate Park, but not sure of exactly where. He scanned the street and stopped when he recognized the church where he had first met Trixie. Then he turned back to the old man, who smelled about as ripe as he looked. Was that a twig sticking out of his beard?

"Do you live under this tree?" Jimmy asked.

"It is a very nice tree, isn't it?" The man's mouth broke into an enthusiastic smile, and he gestured up at the tree behind him.

"So you don't have an ARC then?" Trixie asked, her eyes intent, scanning the man all over as if she were a biologist that had discovered a new species of animal.

The man frowned, vigorously shaking his head from side to side. "Is there not enough drama in the world already?"

Jimmy looked from Trixie to the old man, both of whom appeared to be studying each other with interest. Then he checked his watch. He frowned as he saw the massive crack in the glass. The face was blank.

"What is your name?" Trixie asked.

"My name? The label for this body?" He seemed genuinely surprised at the question and spent a moment in contemplation before answering. "A label defines. How can I put a label on that which is beyond definition?"

"So you don't have a name?" Jimmy rolled his eyes.

"I am all names and yet none. What label can I choose that would not be misleading?"

"What are we supposed to call you then?" Jimmy's words came quickly, impatiently. Trixie could tell that he had little patience for philosophy.

"It does not matter. Call me what you like."

"Fine! I'll call you Crazy Beard then," Jimmy said, throwing his hands up in the air.

"So be it!"

Jimmy leaned over to Trixie and spoke quietly. "This guy is a crazy old fool."

Trixie nodded but said nothing. Crazy, possibly, but he was no fool.

"Come with us," she said.

Crazy Beard's eyes danced as he looked at Trixie, contemplating her request. Then he simply shrugged his shoulders, got up, and dusted the leaves off his clothes with his hands.

Jimmy scanned the man up and down, wrinkling his nose. His inspection lingered on Crazy Beard's dirty bare feet. "We're taking him with us?"

"Yes," Trixie said.

"Why?"

"He can see us."

"So what?"

"If he can see us, then he will remember us." Trixie turned to face Jimmy, speaking in the same tone she would use with a confused toddler. "And if Adam sticks a chip in his head this afternoon, then Adam will have seen and remembered us too. Let's go."

She then turned, starting to walk away. Jimmy watched her back. The old man winked at him and followed after. There seemed to be no tension in his body, and he walked as if he were a carefree child, swinging his arms in an exaggerated motion to keep up with Trixie. Jimmy shook his head and jogged to catch up with them. The three of them walked quietly across the rest of the field, then made their way onto the sidewalk and followed it for a few blocks.

Emergency vehicles sped past, the surrounding traffic automatically parting to create gaps that allowed the trucks through. All vehicles kept moving at their optimal speeds, the maneuvers perfectly synchronized as if all the cars were part of one fluid organism. There was a burning smell that filled the air, and a cloud of black smoke hung in the sky at the other side of the park. A helicopter hovered over the debris of the building, making circles around it.

"Trixie," Jimmy said after he sped up to walk side by side with the young girl in the lead. He had accepted that this was the same Trixie that he had known before, but still had trouble addressing her as such, his voice faltering slightly every time he said her name. "Can I ask you a question?"

Trixie looked at Jimmy, her expression open and curious.

"Can a singularity tell a lie?"

Trixie laughed. "A lie?"

Jimmy looked down, unable to hold eye contact for more than a couple seconds. "From before . . . something Adam said. . . ."

"Of course we can lie." She studied Jimmy's face. He looked at her briefly, then back down at the ground. He didn't seem convinced. She knew there were things that Adam had told him which he hadn't relayed to the others. What was he so worried about?

"Jimmy, one plus one is seventeen. See? A math lie—the worst kind."

Jimmy grinned at her. She smiled back and punched him in the shoulder, not too hard, but hard enough to make him wince and rub the spot. "Big strong football player, getting beat up by a girl. . . ."

FOURTEEN

It was the worst day at the San Francisco Police Headquarters in years. All the officers gathered together in small groups, sharing information and gossip. Only Lieutenant Sanchez sat alone at his desk, the cubby behind him empty. He was one of the few officers not required to share his workspace. It suited him—he had never been much of a talker.

Sanchez ran a shaky hand through the hair on the side of his head, where it was thickest. He still worked out religiously as he had always done, and was always in the top fitness percentile for his age group, but he could no longer ignore the hard truth: he was on the losing end of an unwinnable battle against time. The hair he had left was thin and gray, his joints ached, and wrinkles gathered together in alarming numbers at the corners of his eyes.

To Lieutenant Sanchez, the entire floor sounded like one gigantic beehive, filled with busy buzzing bees. Four officers had lost their lives in the blast this morning. A sadness and anger hovered in the room, but the mourning was only the top layer. He could tell there was more going on than that.

"Sanchez! Did you hear?" The question came from Eric

Smith, a young man who had been with the force less than a year. The sides of his head were trimmed close, with the blond hair on top left long enough to comb to the side. The last remnants of a difficult case of adolescent acne dotted his pale cheeks and forehead.

"Yeah. Crazy, right?"

Officer Smith nodded and scampered off, stopping to listen in on a conversation between three sergeants two cubicles down. Sanchez watched the young man and the three other police officers as they spoke together. He couldn't hear what they were saying, but their faces were animated and they gestured wildly with their hands as they spoke. These were not the actions of officers in mourning.

It was excitement. That was the other emotion. It was the first time many of the younger officers had ever encountered anything like this.

Sanchez had been around long enough to live through the transformation that the SFPD had undergone in recent years. When he had joined the force and paid his dues on the street, he wore a bulletproof vest and carried a firearm. Police work had been different then. Cops had to investigate and solve crimes and arrest the perpetrators. He had been punched, bitten, and shot at in the line of duty. It was a dangerous job.

All of that had changed after congress passed the Universal Crime Prevention Act. Now, solving crimes was as easy as running a search on the ARCNet database. Half the time, the perpetrator's own ARC called 911 and sent the offender online in the middle of committing the act. The police found them staring off into space in the middle of a would-be crime scene, standing there quietly waiting to be arrested. No one committed serious crimes anymore.

Reminder: Your meeting is in five minutes.

The notification startled Sanchez, and he tore his eyes from the officers he had been watching. If ARC was good for anything, it was for keeping him punctual. He hadn't been late for a meeting since he had received his implant.

Reschedule any non-critical appointments this afternoon, he thought at the SFPD central computer. He didn't remember the last time he had a critical appointment. The most pressing issue on his calendar today had been mediating a dispute between two elderly men in a co-housing unit in Chinatown. Apparently, one of them owned a cat that had killed and eaten two of the three parakeets that the other kept as pets. Maybe the delay would give the cat an opportunity to finish his trifecta? It was the closest thing to a serial killing that Sanchez ever expected to see again.

Appointments rescheduled, his chip confirmed.

Sanchez shuffled and stacked some loose papers on his desk and leaned back in his chair. He crossed his feet on his desk, long past the point of trying to look professional at the office, and his eyes unfocused as he joined the meeting.

He found himself in a large circular room. There were four rows of long, curved tables that wrapped around a central podium. Sanchez was seated at his usual spot behind the higher-ups in his department and looked around as he waited for the meeting to begin. It was the largest online briefing room he had been in, and he watched as bodies materialized into the seats around him. The echoed sounds of murmurings and hushed conversations increased in volume as the room filled in. Departments from the entire Bay Area had representatives present.

"All right, people. Let's get this started." The voice was loud and rough. SFPD Chief Munroe was an old timer. Sanchez had known him from high school, and the two had remained close friends over the years. Chief Munroe was a bulldog of a man: short, fat, and uncommonly strong. He was known equally for his uncompromising attitude on the job and his love of home brewing. Officers who found their way into his good graces frequently found themselves gifted with bottles of *Munroe's Original Oatmeal Stout.* Sanchez had received a case every Christmas Day since Munroe had converted his garage to a brewery.

"As you know, there has been a tragedy today. Twenty-two civilians were killed, and over thirty others were injured in the explosion at the Golden Gate Park. In addition, four officers lost their lives in the line of duty." Munroe's voice was gruff and tinged with emotion. He paused and looked around the room. Silence filled the air. No one whispered when the Chief was speaking.

"This was an act of domestic terrorism. Our investigators have linked this act to a terrorist group that has been meeting at the park and planning the attack for the last year and a half."

A picture of the Golden Gate Universal Unitarian church appeared in the air above Munroe, floating there like an apparition. "They met under the pretense of being a twelve-step group for ARC-challenged individuals. This church was where they gathered and where we believe they constructed their explosive devices."

"None of these individuals had ARC implants, which we believe was by design to avoid detection by the authorities. We have been able to reconstruct the group's membership, with help from the ARC of an informant who had unwittingly tried to attend meetings to cope with his disability earlier this year."

A large picture of Cecil took the place of the church. His full name and address appeared underneath his likeness.

"Cecil Coleman the football player?" a voice interrupted from the front row.

Munroe twitched and scowled down at the person who had interrupted him. "Yes. The same."

Sanchez heard a few whispers from behind him from some younger officers.

"I didn't know Cecil Coleman was ARC-challenged."

"Football can really mess with your brain. I won't let my kids play it offline."

Cecil's picture disappeared and was replaced by the pictures of others who had attended the meetings with him. It was a comprehensive list that contained everyone from Cecil's memories who didn't have an ARC. Their names, addresses, and other information floated in the air next to their photos.

"These are terrorists who have committed the highest acts of violence and aggression against an innocent populace," Munroe continued. "Under the Universal Crime Prevention Act, these people do not have the rights of citizens. They are armed and dangerous enemy combatants who have declared war on our country. They killed four of our own, and they intend to engage in more attacks in the immediate future. We're not bringing them in. We're going to kill these vermin."

An angry murmur rippled through the hall. Sanchez felt and recognized it. He knew he wouldn't be tasked with being on the ground in an operation like this but secretly wished that he could be a part of it. Like the others, a thirst for vengeance and justice had quickly flowered in his heart.

"We believe this organization has been recruiting members from the minority non-ARC population in our city and the surrounding areas. We will be rounding up anyone without an ARC for interrogation and mandatory implant surgery, starting immediately. Use caution when approaching anyone without a chip, as some of these individuals may already be compromised.

"Your orders will be delivered to you momentarily. Are there any questions?" Munroe waited, but no one had anything to ask. A restlessness had taken hold of the officers. There was no time to waste on questions. Now was the time for action.

"We've had it easy the last few years, but today the city needs us. It's time for you all to earn those badges. Get out there and kick some ass."

There was a cheer that went up. Chief Munroe surveyed the crowd, his expression fierce.

Lieutenant Sanchez found himself back at his desk. He brought his feet down and stood up to look around. What had been a floor of idle, gossiping individuals only minutes before had transformed itself into a unified team with a driving purpose. Officers rushed down the halls, moving quickly and with determination. Any talking was brief and to the point. Sanchez smiled. After years of feeling obsolete, he finally felt like he had an important job to do. He sat down to review his orders and got to work.

FIFTEEN

The apartment was tiny. There were only two rooms—the main living area, with a compact kitchen and sitting area, and a small bedroom.

"Welcome home," Trixie said, as she held the door open for Jimmy and Crazy Beard.

"Whose place is this?" Jimmy took a quick look around. There were no pictures on the walls, and the apartment had an empty feeling, like no one actually lived there.

"Jenna's."

Trixie reached up and pulled the attachment out of the side of her head, putting it back in one of the zippered pouches in her backpack. She took her baseball cap off and tossed it on the counter.

Jimmy reached up to pull his attachment out, too, but was stopped.

"Leave yours in. Adam knows what you look like."

Jimmy's hand paused in mid-air, then dropped back to his side, leaving the device untouched. He walked over to the fridge and stood in front of it, waiting but nothing happened.

"Some chip upgrade. I can't even talk to the refrigerator." He reached out and pulled the handles open.

"As long as you've got that attachment in, all the normal functions of your chip will be disabled. But, you'll also show up as an error to anyone with an ARC, which makes you as good as invisible. Trust me, you don't want to be seen right now."

Jimmy pulled out a carton of milk and smelled it. He jerked his head back and to the side, then emptied the contents in the sink. As he did so, "Milk" appeared on the shopping list on the front of the door next to a graphic of a milk carton.

"So I'm cut off from society now? I feel naked."

Crazy Beard had made his way over to the couch and tested the spring of the cushion with the tips of his fingers. Satisfied, he arranged himself in the corner, bringing his feet up and crossing his legs under. "We do not bring any clothes with us when we come into this world, and we cannot take any with us when we leave it. We are born naked, and we will die naked. It is our nature to be naked. This is good."

Trixie and Jimmy both looked at Crazy Beard, who only smiled back.

"There's no food," Trixie said. "I'll go get some later."

"So what was the point?"

"Of what?"

"Of talking to Adam."

"The less you know the better."

"You still want to keep secrets?" Jimmy rubbed his temple with two fingers, the headache continued to be an unwelcome guest. "Everyone died. For what? For a five-minute conversation?"

Trixie's lips tightened and her eyes hardened, but she didn't say anything.

"Was it worth it?" Jimmy looked at her.

"Maybe."

"Maybe? What do you mean? Why did everyone have to die?"

Trixie exhaled and looked out the small window across the room. It was a clear day, and the sun sparkled on the sheets of glass on the buildings across the street. They were high enough up in the apartment complex that they couldn't see the street but still too low to have a view of anything except the sides of the other buildings that surrounded them.

"If Adam put an ARC into any of them, which is exactly what he would have done had he gotten a hold of any of us, then he would know . . . everything." Jimmy could tell that Trixie was choosing her words carefully. "They all knew about Jenna's body, and so he would know about Jenna's body too. They knew about the attachments," Trixie pointed at Jimmy's head, "and how they worked. Everything we had built would have been lost. We couldn't let that happen."

Jimmy opened his mouth to speak, but Trixie cut him off. "You knew them for a day, Jimmy. I lived with them my whole life. That was my family that died back there. They sacrificed themselves for me. For you."

Trixie reached up and wiped a tear from her cheek with the back of her hand. In that moment, Jimmy stopped thinking about chips or singularities. He forgot about the explosion. He only saw a young woman that was crying. He took a step toward her, reaching. He wanted to comfort her, to hold her, but was uncertain and awkward in his approach.

Trixie brushed his arms away with a slap of her hand. It felt like someone had cracked a whip against his skin. "You look like shit. Let me find you a hat."

———

Jenna threw the comforter back over her bed. It fell at odd

angles, with one corner almost touching the ground, while the other struggled to barely cover its edge of the mattress. Close enough.

She made her way into the bathroom and studied her face in the mirror. There were dark shadows under her blue eyes, and her skin looked paler than she remembered. She rummaged in a drawer and came out with a brush, which she ran through her long hair a few times in a futile effort to tame it. She tied it in a ponytail and poked the end through the back of her cap, arranging everything to make sure her chip was covered. Her eyes fell upon a lipstick container, but her hand stopped in mid-air as she started to reach for it.

Lipstick? Trixie's question materialized inside her mind, not quite sarcastic, but not approving either.

Jenna withdrew her hand and took a last look at herself in the mirror. The lights automatically dimmed behind her as she left the bathroom. She came to a stop on her way out of the bedroom and spun on her heel to turn back around. Before the bathroom lights had come back on, she was already reaching for the lipstick.

Just a little, she thought, rubbing her lips together in the way she had watched her mother do when applying lipstick. *And maybe just a little gloss too.* She knew Trixie didn't approve, but she didn't care.

When she went out in the living room, she found Jimmy and Crazy Beard sharing a box of cereal. Jimmy held the box, but they were taking turns reaching in and stuffing handfuls of flakes into their mouths. The cushions from the sofa were arranged in a makeshift bed on the floor. It looked like one of them had slept on the cushions, while the other got the sofa. Jimmy wore the baseball cap she had given him yesterday and had it tipped up a little too far—she could still see the corner of his implant.

"Hey. We found some cereal. It's a little stale and dry, but still good," Jimmy said.

"We saved you some," Crazy Beard added with a wide grin, pointing a gnarled finger at a large glass on the table filled to the top with cereal.

Jenna picked up the glass and sat down at the table with the others, munching on the old cereal. She hadn't realized how hungry she was until she started eating. Jimmy topped off her glass after she had made it halfway down and smiled at her.

Crazy Beard got up and nudged a sofa cushion over toward the wall with his foot. He made himself comfortable, crossing his legs as was his custom, and then fell into a deep meditation.

Jimmy and Jenna watched him for a moment, silently finishing their breakfast.

"He might as well have an ARC. The only difference is that he closes his eyes," Jenna said.

"Are you sure he doesn't?"

He doesn't.

"Trixie says he doesn't."

Jimmy started at her words and looked at Jenna as if he had just met her. "So, you're not Trixie now?"

Jenna giggled. "No. Just Jenna. But she's in here too."

Jimmy offered his hand, and the two shook. "Hi, Jenna. I'm Jimmy." His hand was warm and much larger than hers.

"I know who you are, silly."

"Oh, sorry." Jimmy looked at her quietly for a moment. "So what is it like? I mean, when Trixie, you know . . . when Trixie drives."

Jenna smiled, amused at Jimmy's efforts to try to ask the question politely. "It's like a dream. I'm there, and I know what is happening, but I'm not in control. It was strange at first, but now I'm used to it."

Jimmy nodded, listening. "So I've been meaning to ask . . . do you work out?"

"That's a weird question."

Jimmy blushed. "Sorry. It's just that twice now, once with the dark-haired, rocker girl and—"

"That was Trisha. She was my cousin."

"Oh. Once with Trisha and . . . ," Jimmy's voice trailed off as he watched Jenna wither under the name of her cousin. "I'm really sorry about her, by the way."

"Thanks." Jenna felt a lump in her throat and looked down. The heartbreak of losing Trisha and the others came rushing back to the surface.

Jimmy stopped and waited for a moment, watching Jenna. Eventually, after her emotions had subsided, he continued. "So once with Trisha and then once with you, you both were really strong. Like too strong."

Jenna nodded. "Yeah, that's Trixie. She knows how to do that."

The human body is built to allow for hysterical strength. Usually it only happens in life and death situations, like when a mother needs to lift a car off her child to save him. Obviously, it can also be harnessed for other purposes if you know what strings to pull in the brain.

"She says the body is built to do it. It's called . . ." *What was it called?*

Hysterical strength.

". . . hysterical strength. She knows how to make it happen."

"That's handy. I hope we don't have to arm wrestle any time soon. . . ."

Jenna laughed.

I'd kick your ass, Jimmy Mahoney.

The two were silent then. Jenna glanced up at Jimmy, who was staring out the window with a far-off look in his eye. He was more sturdy than handsome, especially with the day-old scruff on his face, but there was a warmth about him that was undeniable. Jenna had felt it from the beginning. She lowered her gaze to take in his broad shoulders and made her way down his arm to linger on the gold wedding ring on his finger. Her heart began to pound.

"So Trixie says we only have a 50-50 chance of living through the next couple days . . . ," Jenna said.

"That's nice to hear."

Actually, it's worse than that.

"Actually, worse than 50-50."

"Gets better all the time!"

"And so. I was wondering . . ."

"What?"

Just tell him.

Give me a minute.

"It might be the end of the world. I mean not literally, but like maybe the end of humanity. And we might be dead tomorrow."

"I know."

"And so if there's anything we never got a chance to do. Well, maybe we should, you know, do those things . . ."

Jimmy furrowed his eyebrows. "What do you mean?"

Jenna exhaled and looked away.

Trisha used to work at BioCal and had known about Adam from the beginning. She had seen his true nature, and along with Randall and Chris, had been among the first to go underground. She was the one that had brought Jenna onboard, to save her. Jenna had only been sixteen at the time. She never had a chance to really be a teenager. While her old friends were busy dating and getting asked to prom, she spent most of her time networked to a singularity, sleeping on a cot and doing research. What was it like to have a boyfriend? What did it feel like to be kissed? She didn't know. She might never know. And now, it was too late. Every man that she met had an ARC in his head. Every man she ever saw on the street had a devil inside of him. Except for Jimmy. Who was married. And probably too old for her anyway.

"Never mind," Jenna said, standing up then rushing over to the front door. "I should probably go get some food. Stay here until I get back." Then she left.

Jimmy stared after her, confused. When it was clear that she wasn't coming back, he turned to find Crazy Beard watching him and smiling mischievously. "Ah, spring! When a young man's fancy turns to thoughts of love."

SIXTEEN

Jenna skipped down the stairs two at a time. She didn't want to wait for the elevator and moving always helped work out her nerves. She reached the ground floor and pushed through the door to emerge on the sidewalk.

The sun felt good on her face, and she stopped to close her eyes and soak it in. She took a deep breath. Standing there in the warmth, listening to the quiet hum of traffic, she could almost pretend that yesterday hadn't happened and that this was just another beautiful spring day in the city. But the illusion was fleeting and lasted only until Trixie interrupted her.

You're wasting time.

Jenna sighed and opened her eyes. She walked down the sidewalk and across the street. She knew of a grocery store four or five blocks away, where she would be able to pick up supplies.

Jenna had left her attachment in the backpack. Trixie had felt it was safer to avoid using it if at all possible. Being invisible was good for escaping a mob but dangerous otherwise, especially in a big city with lots of people and traffic. No one knew about Jenna. To the outside world, she was just another person on the street.

Jimmy, on the other hand, was different. Trixie wanted to leave his attachment in all day and night and never let him out of the apartment. He was the key to making all of this work, and now Adam knew about him.

Does Adam think Jimmy is dead? Jenna asked.

Probably. But he's still going to look for him anyway.

For how long?

I don't know. Fifty years? Forever?

Jenna rushed across the street, cutting over through the gap between two clusters of traffic. This side of the street was still in the shadow, and she felt the temperature drop dramatically.

He's not going to be able to see his wife again, is he?

No.

Jenna reached the corner and stopped walking. To get out of the way of others, she stepped sideways and stood off to the side by a trash receptacle. A rotten banana peel hung over the edge of the garbage, half in and half out. Two flies danced over the bin, circling each other with a quiet hum of tiny wings.

We tricked him, didn't we?

There's more at stake here than Jimmy.

But we did! We offered him a way to be with his wife again, and we did the opposite.

Things didn't happen the way we planned.

They were in love. He just wanted to be with her. And now he can never see her again. Jenna wiped her eyes. She felt like all she ever did anymore was cry. *Trixie, we're such assholes!*

Trixie laughed. *Yeah, we kind of are.* The buzzing in the center of Jenna's head tickled her nose. She always felt like sneezing when Trixie laughed.

It's not funny.

We're in a war, Jenna. Adam took Jimmy's wife from him a long time ago. As bad as it looks right now, we are still his best chance of getting her back.

Jenna rummaged in her pocket, looking for a tissue, but couldn't find one. She wiped her eyes off with her hands and rubbed them on the legs of her pants.

Good thing you didn't decide to wear mascara with that lipstick.

You are impossible.

It was only two more blocks to the grocery store. The sliding glass doors automatically parted to let Jenna enter. It was a small store on the corner, with eight aisles and an almost-miniature produce section. But despite the limited floor space, Jenna had always been able to find everything she needed. She used to always try to shop on Wednesdays, since that's when the store offered free doughnuts in the back. Jenna knew it wasn't the right day but glanced at the back of the store anyway, just in case. Instead of doughnuts, the table held a stack of paper towels arranged in a pyramid, with a handwritten "buy one, get one free" sign on pink paperboard.

Jenna took hold of a small red cart and made her way down the aisles, grabbing various items as she went. Peanut butter, chips, a bag of red licorice, more cereal. . . . She didn't have a list and selected items by reflex rather than by plan. She knew it was impossible to forget anything important with Trixie watching.

Don't forget the milk.

Jenna made her way to the back of the store, and the glass barrier between her and the milk slid to the side as she reached in and grabbed a carton. It quietly moved back into place once her hand was withdrawn.

When she turned back around, there were two police officers standing behind her.

"Oh!" Jenna said with a start. She wasn't paying attention and hadn't heard anyone come up behind her.

"Sorry to startle you, ma'am," the officer on the left said. He was younger than his partner, but taller and more muscular. He held a strange device in his hand that looked like an old-fashioned phone. It had a screen that displayed various words and colored icons, but Jenna couldn't make any of it out with just a glance. The officer next to him had gray hair and an oversized midsection which looked like it would be difficult to fasten a tactical belt around. She noticed that his hand was resting lightly on the top of his holstered weapon.

Just play dumb, Trixie said.

"How can I help you?" Jenna said, looking from one officer to the next, but addressing the one that had spoken first.

"Pursuant to policies adopted after the recent terrorist attack in the Golden Gate Park, we've been ordered to detain and question anyone suspicious who might have information about the criminal gang that perpetrated the event."

"Terrorist attack?"

"Yes, ma'am," the younger officer said. "Over twenty people were killed yesterday."

"Can you please tell us your name, ma'am?" the older officer asked.

"My name? Why?"

The young officer looked down at the device in his hand, waving it past Jenna in a circle. "You don't appear to have an ARC implant. Is that correct?"

"No, I never got one. . . ."

The older officer's hand moved from resting on the top of his gun, down to grasp the grip. He loosened it in the holster but didn't draw it.

"Your name, ma'am," the older officer asked again. There was a harshness in his voice. Jenna recognized her stepfather in the firm, commanding tone. This was not a man that was used to being disobeyed without consequences.

"It's Jennifer . . . Jennifer Smith." Jenna made up a last name.

"I'm afraid you'll need to come with us, Miss Smith," the younger officer said. He slipped his device into a fitted pouch on his belt and snapped a leather fastener over the top to lock it into place.

"Why?"

"I'm sorry, but we've got orders to bring in every non-ARC resident in the city for routine questioning."

Questioning, my ass. More like to put an ARC in your head. Adam is tying up loose ends. That was a scanner he had.

"But I didn't do anything! I'm just out grocery shopping."

The officer reached for a pair of handcuffs, which flicked open on their own as he withdrew them from their place at his side. His partner had drawn his weapon, but kept it pointed at the ground.

"You aren't in any trouble, ma'am, but your compliance is not optional. Please turn around and place your hands behind your back," the younger officer said. His voice was calm, but his eyes were hard.

Jenna's eyes darted from the face of one man to the other and then fell upon the handcuffs, open and ready to accept her wrists. They were going to arrest her! Her mouth went dry, and she could feel her own heartbeat hammering against the sides of her throat. A surge of adrenaline hit her hard in the chest. Thousands of years of fight-or-flight evolution in her genes was screaming one thing at her as loud as it could: Run!

Trixie, I need you!

SEVENTEEN

Officers Rudy Parker and Tony MacGuire stepped out of the elevator and into a dimly lit hallway. It took a second before the lights in the ceiling responded to their presence, which was a common cost-cutting measure for apartment complexes in this price range. As they walked down the hall, the lights ahead of them flickered on at the same time the ones they had just passed dimmed.

"How do we know anyone is even in this place?" Rudy asked his partner.

"The fridge says someone threw out some milk."

"The fridge?!" Rudy snorted. "So now we're checking in on kitchen appliances?"

Tony laughed. "The damned things are smarter than my kids, but they still don't throw out their own rotten milk. The analysts think there's someone in there without a chip."

Rudy grunted. He didn't like the analysts, but he knew how successful they were at solving crimes. It still felt like a waste of his time. A full-blown terrorist attack had just happened, and here he was sent to investigate a refrigerator.

The two stopped at a dirty gray door. Four metal numbers

had been nailed to the wall on the right side of the doorway: this was unit 1113. The final number 3 had lost a fastener and was angled sharply away from the other numbers, trying to escape. The numbers looked like they had once been shiny but were now dirty and old.

"I'll bet you an Oatmeal Stout that no one is in there," Rudy said.

Tony had been reaching up to knock on the door and stopped abruptly. "Are you serious? One of Munroe's? How the fuck did you ever get your hands on a Munroe's Original?"

Rudy smiled, his eyes twinkling. "Sanchez came to poker night last week, and we cleaned him out. The old bastard can't bluff for shit."

Tony howled loudly, slapping his thigh and bending over. His eyes were watering when he finally stopped laughing to come up for air. "You got him to bet his Originals? God, that's classic. You know he's never going to play with you again."

"He'll get over it. He's probably got enough of Munroe's beer to fill up a bathtub."

"Probably." Tony rolled his eyes, then turned his attention back to the door. He cleared his throat and banged on the door with his fist three times. "Police! Open up!"

The two waited five seconds, but the door remained closed.

Sergeant Tony MacGuire with San Francisco Police, serving a warrant to enter the premises, Tony thought at the door. There was a click as the lock opened, and he reached out and pushed the door open.

————

Jimmy was sitting on the sofa, staring absentmindedly out the window. He had moved one of the sofa cushions back up from the floor to sit on, but Crazy Beard had kept the other one.

Crazy Beard had spent the entire morning sitting on that cushion, legs crossed. As far as Jimmy could figure, the old man was spending his time staring at the wall. Crazy Beard's eyes were open, but his look was far away and he never blinked. At first, Jimmy had tried to play a game and see if he could hold his eyes open longer than Crazy Beard but hadn't lasted long. He didn't see Crazy Beard blink even once.

Jimmy looked down at his watch, forgetting that it was broken. He grunted quietly as he looked down at the cracked screen. Where was Jenna? He had so many questions he wanted to ask.

There was a noise in the hallway. It sounded like it was coming from right outside the door. Voices. Male voices. And laughter. Jimmy looked at the inside of the door. He felt his heart rate begin to increase. Was someone at the door?

Bam-Bam-Bam!

"Police! Open up!"

Jimmy leapt from the sofa. The police? Crazy Beard was no longer looking at the wall but had turned his head toward the door, a quizzical look on his face.

Jimmy seized the old man by the arm and hauled him up off the ground.

"Quick! We have to hide," Jimmy whispered through clenched teeth. But where? The apartment was tiny. He looked around, searching wildly. There was nowhere to hide.

There was the sound of metal on metal as the lock in the door opened.

Jimmy dragged Crazy Beard into the bedroom. He shut the door behind them, taking care to close it as quietly as he could without slowing down.

There was a small bed, one side table, and a closet. A door led to the only bathroom in the apartment; there wasn't even a shower curtain to hide behind in there.

He rushed to the window and looked out. They were halfway up a very tall building. The street was a long way down, and there was nothing to stand on outside the window. Jimmy considered trying to hang by his hands from the windowsill but immediately discarded the idea as suicidal. No escape.

There was a space under the bed. He would never fit. Crazy Beard might though.

"Under the bed!" Jimmy whispered.

Crazy Beard looked down, then back at Jimmy. "This body can fit in many places, but that doesn't look like one of them."

"No time. Just get under there. Hurry!" Jimmy pushed Crazy Beard down and lifted the end of the bed up so he could quickly get himself positioned. Jimmy then lowered the bed back down on top of the man. Crazy Beard grunted. The bottom leg of the frame barely touched the ground—it was too tight a fit. There was no time to do anything about it.

"Hello? San Francisco Police!" the voices came from the other room.

"Tony, look."

"I see it."

What did they see? The cushions? The box of cereal? Jimmy spun wildly. Where to hide?

He threw open the closet door and flung himself inside. Like everything else in the apartment, the closet was too small. He fought with the clothes, trying to make space for himself next to them. He stumbled over a pile of shoes on the floor and ended up half-crouched on top of them. He tried to pull the door closed but couldn't get it shut.

Jimmy heard the bedroom door creak open. He held his breath. His heart was pounding in his ears.

Someone laughed.

"Are you kidding?"

"How did you even get under there?" another voice said. "Come on, get out."

"This body is stuck," Crazy Beard said. There was a strain in his voice.

There was a sound of furniture being moved. Jimmy tried to peek through the crack in the closet door but couldn't see anything.

"Do you want to scan him?"

"Yeah. Hold on. . . ." There was a sound of something unsnapping, then a pause. "I'll be damned. No ARC. They were right."

"Told you. Refrigerators are coming for your job, Rudy."

Laughter.

"Bathroom's clear. Check the closet."

Jimmy froze. He pulled the edge of a hanging sweater sideways, trying to cover his face.

The closet door opened, and a rough hand threw the sweater aside. An olive-skinned officer stood in the doorway. He was dressed in a navy uniform, and the bulletproof vest strapped over his chest only added to his already burly physique. He looked right at Jimmy, then across to the other side of the closet.

The man held the closet door open wide, as he turned back around to face the other officer, who watched from the middle of the room. "Nothing in the closet. Just the guy under the bed."

Jimmy saw Crazy Beard sitting on the bed. His hands were restrained behind him, held in place by a thick pair of silver handcuffs. His face was red, but he was smiling. He made eye contact with Jimmy and winked.

The officer closed the door, but it hit Jimmy in the leg and bounced back open. He tried closing it a second time with more force, and Jimmy bit his lip as the door smashed hard against him. It sprung back open again. There was a curse.

"Just leave it."

The closet door was closed halfway, and Jimmy heard footfalls echo on the hard floor. The officers had left the bedroom. There was the sound of a door closing from the other room, then silence.

Jimmy exhaled. He struggled to extricate himself from the morass of shoes that he was stuck in but was unable to get out of the closet without tripping over the end of a boot. The bed sat at a strange angle to the walls, left out of place after the police had lifted it off Crazy Beard. He had to shuffle-step around a corner in his effort to get past.

Jimmy quietly approached the bedroom door and softly pulled it open. He paused, listening, but heard nothing. He poked his head into the living room. It was empty. They were gone.

He rushed to the front door and reached for the knob, but hesitated. He put his head flat against the door, listening. He couldn't hear anything. As quietly as he could, he turned the knob and opened the door just a crack. No one was there. He risked opening it more and caught a glimpse of the officers.

They were halfway down the hall toward the elevators, their backs toward him. Crazy Beard walked between them, his hands cuffed behind his back. One of the officers had a hand on his upper arm, guiding him forward.

Jimmy shut the door. They had Crazy Beard and were taking him away. What should he do? He tore through the kitchen, searching for paper and a pen. There was nothing. Aside from the half-eaten box of cereal on the counter, the kitchen was sparse. How would he tell Trixie what had happened?

He seized the cereal box, looking inside. Write a message with flakes of cereal? This was all he had. But it was a stupid idea. There was no time.

"Think, Jimmy!" he said aloud. He gave himself one second. No bright ideas came. It wasn't right for them to swoop in and take Crazy Beard like they did. That much he knew. He felt it in his gut. He had to try to do something. But what?

"You're invisible. They can't see you." Jimmy placed a hand on the doorknob, and took a breath to calm his nerves, closing his eyes as he did so. Then, he quietly cracked the door open and slipped out into the hallway.

EIGHTEEN

"Ma'am, I need you to turn around and put your hands behind your back," the officer told Trixie. He had a pair of handcuffs out and took a step toward her. Her half-filled shopping cart was between them, and the officer put one hand on it to pull it out of the way. Trixie held the handle firm, keeping it in place.

"Don't make this harder than it needs to be. We don't want to have to hurt you," the older officer next to him said. His tongue flicked the corner of his mouth, like a snake. He had taken his pistol out of its holster but hadn't pointed it at Trixie yet. There was a hard edge in his voice, and she could hear the undertones that told her more than his words did: he was enjoying this. This officer was old and out of shape compared to his younger partner, but she had no doubt which one was more dangerous.

Despite their apparent advantage in size and numbers, she knew the two officers had made a critical mistake. They had underestimated her. They thought she was weak and scared. They would soon learn how wrong they were.

With the quickness of a tigress, Trixie grabbed a hold of the end of the peanut butter container in the shopping basket and flipped it up at the young officer across from her. He was barely able to turn his head to the side before the glass jar smashed into the side of his face, sending him reeling backward.

The older officer's eyes went wide, and he tried to raise his gun, but Trixie was on him before he could train it on her. She moved like a dancer, with effortless speed and perfect efficiency. There was no movement out of place or even an ounce of wasted energy. It was as if she was in a recital, performing a choreographed set of motions that she had rehearsed a thousand times before.

Trixie's left hand wrapped around the top of the barrel of the officer's pistol and her right came down in an arc, slapping the man hard in the face as she found her way to the back of the gun, on top of the officer's own hand. Having both ends of the weapon between her hands, she pushed with her left and pulled with her right in a quick motion that wrenched the pistol free. The officer screamed as the movement bent his finger backward, breaking it against the edge of the trigger guard.

Trixie maintained her momentum and spun to club the younger officer with the handle of his partner's weapon. There was a crunching sound as she connected with his skull. She knew that the gun was only useful to her as a blunt instrument; its automatic safety wouldn't disengage for anyone but the registered owner.

Trixie turned her attention back to the older officer and stomped the side of his knee with her heel, forcing him to the ground. She then cracked him over the head with his own gun, knocking him into an unconscious heap.

She knew she had to be quick. These officers both had ARCs, and they had both seen her face. If she wanted to maintain a shred of anonymity, she couldn't let Adam gain access to their memories. It might already be too late.

Trixie looked back at the younger officer. He was sprawled

on the ground, his face covered in peanut butter and blood. They had both been knocked out, but they would recover and they would remember. She knew she had to finish it. She moved over the officer's prone body and reached down to take hold of the sides of his neck. All it would take would be a quick snap and it would be done.

Then she saw the boy at the end of the aisle.

He couldn't have been more than eight or nine years old. He wore a pair of red overalls, and his face was covered in chocolate ice cream. He held a cone in his hand, but the scoop that had been on it had fallen and rested on the floor at his feet in a brown puddle. He was staring at her, his eyes wide and his mouth open in shock. He had seen everything.

Trixie knew that she had to kill anyone who had been involved in the fight, and that included anyone who had seen it up close. The boy was old enough to have an ARC. All the kids had them. That meant he had to be eliminated too.

She knew what she had to do, but she hesitated, only staring back into those young eyes, which could never be as innocent and carefree as they had once been only minutes ago. The boy and the two officers needed to be killed, and quickly. It was logical. It's what Adam would have done in her shoes. He'd have already finished it. But she wasn't Adam.

"Shit."

Trixie ran.

NINETEEN

The query came back negative.

Broaden the geographical parameters and rerun the search, Adam instructed.

Negative. No matches have been found for any permutations within two hundred miles.

How was that possible? How could a young woman incapacitate two experienced police officers, then disappear as if she never existed? Not a single memory of her could be found in anyone within a two hundred-mile radius of the grocery store at the time of the attack.

Given the distribution of eyes on the ground at the time of the incident, what are the odds of this happening by random chance?

Zero, the thread responded. *There was 93% visual coverage of the area. The zones that were not under direct observation did not intersect and have all been searched since the incident.*

A paradox. The woman could not have passed out of view of everyone with an ARC in the area, and yet that is exactly what had happened. Adam did not believe in paradoxes. Everything was logical and ultimately could be reduced to a series of true and false statements at the most basic level. Mathematical certainty governed the Universe and everything within it. Any paradox simply pointed out missing information or incorrect base assumptions. There was something here that he wasn't aware of. Something important.

Using all available information from the incident, build a profile and cross reference against the database of known locations of independent nodes. Expand search to include records before the incident. Sort by recent activity.

The thread paused as it compiled the results. *Linked sightings of a possible match have been found in records prior to the incident.*

Various memories rapidly flashed through Adam's consciousness. A blond woman with a black baseball cap had crossed the street a block away from the grocery store. Then she was standing on a corner, by a garbage can. Another street crossing. She was walking down the sidewalk. Then standing outside an apartment complex. Then exiting the building. Now it was a different day, and she wore different clothes. She was walking down the hall. Then placing wet clothes in a dryer in the basement laundromat. Saying hello to a neighbor. Now she was smiling at an older woman, helping her with two bags of groceries. They talked about the weather. Jogging. Waiting for the bus.

The suspect rents an apartment under the name Jenna Cappetti. Unit 1113. There is a 99% probability that the name she offered to authorities was a fabrication.

A pause.

Further coincidental information has been identified, the thread stated.

Continue.

An independent node has been recently apprehended within the domicile registered to Jenna Cappetti. Identity unknown.

The thread replayed images of Crazy Beard being pulled

out from under the bed and fast-forwarded through the time he was escorted out of the room by the police. The entire information burst took a fraction of a second, as it was sped up to run over one thousand times faster than actually recorded.

Adam considered the old man's unusual appearance and interactions with authorities during the arrest. *This node appears to be mentally compromised.*

The node's actions do not conform to any standard behavioral profiles. There is a high probability of defective hardware.

Cross reference against other high-priority threads.

The thread paused, interacting with its own sub-threads, as well as other processes running within Adam's expanded frame of awareness. *This node was placed within the Golden Gate Park at the time of the recent incursion by the rogue singularity. He appears in 82% of records as being located under the same tree in the park.*

He lives under a tree? Verify. Extend search back one year.

Confirmed.

So an apparently mentally challenged vagrant, who lives under a tree in the park, has found himself under arrest in the apartment of Jenna Cappetti? The same Jenna Cappetti who inexplicably vanished out of Adam's awareness after attacking and nearly killing two police officers nearly twice her size?

Adam didn't need to ask for an analysis, as the thread had already computed the probabilities for him. *There is a 0.001% probability that this node was in the suspect's apartment by random chance.*

Search for records of these two nodes being in close proximity to each other. Full database query, no constraints.

The thread remained silent, working on its task. Adam usually tried to avoid running open-ended database queries. They required accessing and sifting through every node's complete memory records, which was an inefficient expense that interfered with all his other running processes. Such a directed search tended to focus the network in a way that unified the emotions of all the nodes, which never felt good, especially if the content was difficult. In this case, there wasn't much of an emotional charge around either of the two subjects he was searching for, and so he only felt a brief strain as a wave passed through ARCNet and the subconscious minds of every node connected to it.

No records located.

If the nameless vagrant had never met Jenna Cappetti, then how had he gained access to her apartment? On the same day that she had managed to elude an entire city full of witnesses? On the day after the rogue singularity had violated ARCNet? He didn't need to calculate the odds that these were coincidental anomalies, as he already knew them: zero. One paradox is a puzzling curiosity. Multiple paradoxes are something else entirely.

Assumption: The rogue singularity, the vagrant, and Jenna Cappetti are related. Hypothesize relationship.

A new thread emerged from the blackness in response to Adam's request. *The most logical explanation is that Jenna Cappetti is a surviving node of the singularity.* As the thread reported this, a connection was automatically established between it and the other thread currently in charge of conducting a search for the singularity under the assumption that it had survived the explosion. *The vagrant is either a new node she is attempting to deploy or contains information that she desires or is trying to conceal. No other hypotheses have significant levels of confidence to consider.*

There it was.

She has survived.

Yes, she is resourceful. This is not unexpected.

It was true: Adam hadn't expected her to be destroyed in the explosion. He had hoped for it, perhaps, but not expected it. The simulations he had run had told him that much. Only the most simpleminded of singularities would not have had the foresight to establish an emergency survival strategy under that scenario, and she was clearly anything but simpleminded.

How many nodes does she have left?

Her inability to remain concealed suggests that her network and resources are limited. There is not enough information available to estimate an exact number with confidence.

She has found a way to evade detection.

Clearly the exploit of a vulnerability in either the visual-processing or image-recognition routines.

Debug the affected interfaces and roll out an update once the defect has been identified. Highest priority.

There was only one way to know for certain the extent of the rogue singularity's network: he had to capture one of her nodes and implant an ARC. Jenna Cappetti would do nicely. He even knew where she lived.

TWENTY

Jimmy didn't have a problem running fast. He had once made a career out of doing just that. But running fast and running fast without making any noise are two different skills. He slowed, trying to muffle the sounds of his footfalls.

As he passed under them, lights in the hallway blinked on at the same time as those behind him clicked off.

The two officers were almost to the elevator at the end of the hallway. Crazy Beard walked sandwiched between them, his wrists in cuffs, his upper arm in the grip of one of the men. The three of them all turned around, looking back down the hallway.

Jimmy came to a halt and froze. Had they heard him? His heart pounded and his lungs wanted air, but he fought to keep silent. The light above shined down on him like a spotlight. He hadn't considered the lights. He looked up, then back at the officers. They peered down the hall at him, their brows wrinkled. Crazy Beard looked right at him and laughed out loud.

Quick! Do something! Jimmy took a hesitant step forward, then another. A different light illuminated and the other dimmed. Then he stepped back, reversing the process.

"This place is falling apart," the large olive-skinned officer said, shaking his head.

"Come on," the other said to Crazy Beard and gave him a shove toward the elevator, without releasing his grip. The old man stumbled but caught himself.

"That which is most important is always overlooked by a mind distracted with worldly thoughts. The greatest jewel is hidden in plain sight." Crazy Beard glanced back over his shoulder, his eyes full of mirth.

"This guy is a trip."

"First time you've ever arrested a fortune cookie?"

The two laughed and continued toward the elevator. Jimmy allowed himself a breath, then moved forward as fast and quietly as he could, wincing each time one of the lights came on above him.

The elevator doors opened, and the officers stepped through, pushing Crazy Beard ahead of them. Jimmy sprinted forward, then stopped as the two turned back around to face him. He stood at the edge of the hallway looking in at the three of them, and they stood in the middle of the elevator looking out. Jimmy felt sweat running down the side of his face. He was hot under his shirt. The elevator doors began to close.

Jimmy stuck out his hand to block the doors, and they opened again.

"What the heck?" The officer looked up and down the side of the elevator door.

"Opportunity must not be neglected, for it may never come again," Crazy Beard said to Jimmy.

"I tried that line on my wife last night, but it didn't work. She still didn't want to have sex."

"At least offer her one of your Originals first. She's not going to want to have sex with you if she's not drunk."

"Man. Story of my life."

More laughter.

Jimmy looked from Crazy Beard to the two cops. What to do? There was no time to think, only to act. He took a breath, gathered his courage, then stepped forward into the elevator. The doors closed behind him.

Almost as soon as he had done it, Jimmy regretted his decision. It was a small elevator, and he flattened himself against the doors. The metal doors were smooth and cold against his body. He remembered Trixie's warning not to touch anyone when they had made their way through the crowd. He was inches from either officer. It was too close, but there was nowhere else to stand. He could smell the aftershave on the man to his right, could almost taste the coffee on his breath. The word "Parker" was stitched into the front of his thick navy vest.

"As vast as the Universe and yet small enough to fit inside an atom. Is not the Self astounding?" Crazy Beard said to Jimmy with a smile.

"Is he going to do that the whole time?"

"I think there's a string that you pull to make it happen."

The elevator came to a halt with a bounce, and a chime played as the doors opened. Jimmy tried to back out but stopped himself just as he was about to run into a woman carrying a small child on her hip. The child had curly red hair and looked at Jimmy with inquisitive blue eyes.

Jimmy couldn't go forward and couldn't go back, so he squatted down to try to stay out of the line of vision. The child's eyes followed him, and the young girl squealed.

"I'm sorry, ma'am, it's a little crowded in here. It might be better to take the next one," the large officer said.

"Oh! Yes, I think so," the woman said, stepping back half a step. Her eyes darted between the officers and Crazy Beard, taking in the situation.

"Mommy, what's he doing?" the little girl said in a voice that was entirely too loud. She pointed at Jimmy. Jimmy realized with horror that the girl didn't have an ARC. She was too young.

"Those are police officers, sweetie," the mother said in a sing-song voice. She bounced the child twice, readjusting her position.

"No. What's *he* doing?" the child pointed emphatically at Jimmy.

The elevator doors began to close but caught Jimmy's knee, which was protruding out into the hallway. The doors opened again.

"Again?" Officer Parker said.

"Him? He's being arrested. He's a bad man," the mother said. She gave Crazy Beard a stern glance, but he smiled sweetly back at her.

"Don't you worry. We've got him, and we're taking him away," the large officer said to the girl, speaking slowly to make sure she understood.

"No!" the girl screamed. Jimmy could see the frustration in her eyes as she looked at him, pointing violently with her finger. "What's he doing!?"

Jimmy held up a hand to her and waved it back and forth with a smile, but the action had the opposite effect from what he had hoped, and the girl became even more agitated and started screaming.

"Hush, now. It's ok. Everything's ok," the mother said, bouncing the child on her hip.

The elevator doors began to close a second time, and Jimmy spun his knee out of the way and stood up, making sure to keep the path between the doors clear. He had to stand up in between the mother and the officers, blocking their view of each other, and he looked back and forth trying to tell if they noticed. They didn't seem to. Only the young girl could see him and was doing her best to try to get the adults around her to see him as well. She was screaming and thrashing in her mother's arms, tears running down the sides of her small face, her finger pointed accusingly at Jimmy.

"No! Him!"

The doors closed. The floor of the elevator lurched, and Jimmy felt a rush through his body as it resumed its descent. He felt the perspiration dripping down his torso under his shirt.

"This is kind of a weird apartment building," the large officer said, turning to Parker.

Jimmy watched the officer's face and saw a flicker in the side of his eye. The man frowned and turned his head toward the doors that Jimmy had plastered his body against. The other officer did the same. They both had questioning expressions on their faces, their brows furrowed. Slowly, as if a mist were being lifted, their eyes began to focus.

They both leapt back in shock.

"Holy shit!" Officer Parker exclaimed.

Jimmy felt the bottom fall out of his stomach. Both officers were looking right at him. They could see him. The large olive-skinned officer reached for his gun.

TWENTY-ONE

The four men entered the building in the back, piling into the service elevator. Each was dressed in a black tactical uniform, complete with a bulletproof vest and helmet. "SWAT" was printed in large white letters across their backs.

The elevator doors closed.

Eleventh floor, Officer Jeremiah Jacobs thought, and the elevator groaned as it began its ascent.

The four didn't say anything to each other on the ride up. There was a nervous energy in the air. Aside from the two units called to the site of the terrorist attack yesterday, this was the first live action SWAT had seen in over two years.

Jeremiah never expected to be called out for a real-world emergency again, yet here he was, riding up an elevator on a mission to apprehend a hostile fugitive. He had seen the footage. He knew what their target was capable of, nearly killing two officers with her bare hands in a grocery store.

The elevator came to a stop, and the doors opened.

We've reached the eleventh floor. Moving toward the apartment, Jeremiah thought.

Understood. Keep me posted, the words came back from SWAT Captain Richards.

The team made its way down the hall and came to a stop in front of apartment 1 1 1 3. Jeremiah stood back and let the others take their positions on either side of the door. Their target might hold the key to unraveling the terrorist organization responsible for the attack in the Golden Gate Park, and their orders were to bring her in alive. Their weapons were loaded with non-lethal stun rounds.

We're in position outside the door. Preparing to breach.

Copy.

The door unlocked itself on command, and one SWAT officer pushed it open while the others swept the room to make sure it was clear. The team rushed into the apartment as a unit and flowed over the first room and into the bedroom. They had trained in breaching and clearing rooms together until it had become second nature.

As they expected, the apartment was empty. It hadn't been long since Officers MacGuire and Parker had already been there.

Jeremiah felt the anxiety level drop noticeably, and the team members visibly relaxed. The first half of the operation was a success. They had made their way into the apartment before the target had arrived.

We're in. The apartment is clear.

Confirmed.

The couch was arranged to directly face the door, and two of the men sat down on it, their weapons resting lightly in their hands. The third member of the team pulled a chair from the table and spun it around to face the door. He placed it off to the side and sat down, laying his shotgun across his knees.

Jeremiah didn't feel like sitting, so he leaned against the kitchen counter. He held a large, black electroshock weapon in his hands. In training, he had been on the receiving end of a shock weapon just like this. It had locked up every muscle in his body, completely incapacitating him, and had been the most painful five seconds in his life. Whoever walked through that door next was going to receive a full-charge blast right in the chest, no questions asked.

Captain Richards's voice entered his mind. *Stay alert. Remember, this is a high-value target, and we need her alive.*

Understood, Captain.

TWENTY-TWO

As Trixie ran, she flipped her backpack off her shoulder and worked her hand into one of the zippered pockets. She dodged through the aisles and out the front door of the grocery store. Her hand closed around the device she was looking for, and she stopped to push her cap up and snap the attachment into her chip.

Things hadn't gone the way she had hoped. The two police officers would not have been able to arrest her unless she let them, but something worse than the fight had happened: she had been seen. The look on the boy's face lingered in her memory. There was shock in his eyes. And fear.

Would Adam connect her actions today with her actions yesterday? He had no way to know that Jenna and Trisha were related in any way. But how often does someone without an ARC attack the police? Never. And to do so the day after a group of non-ARC individuals blew up a building? Adam was the most powerful supercomputer of all time, and she knew he was looking for her. It's not like he wouldn't notice the coincidence. She might as well have been waving a huge red flag.

A woman approached. She was walking toward the

entrance to the store, and it was clear she couldn't see Trixie. Trixie moved aside to let her pass.

She could hear sirens. More police were coming.

Trixie looked both ways and dashed across the street. She weaved through the flow of oncoming pedestrian traffic, dodging in and out through the spaces between people. She made sure not to touch anyone. There was no reason to give Adam any more curious data points than she already had.

She stopped in front of a shop with a dirty front door that was propped open. The inside was dimly lit, and she could see rows of liquor bottles and a display of cigars. A balding man sat at the counter by the door, staring at the wall across from him. There was a vacant look in his eyes. Clearly, he was online.

Trixie stepped inside, her eyes fixed on a jar on the counter that held individually wrapped strips of beef jerky. She grabbed two handfuls and stuffed them into her backpack. She topped it off with a box of mints, placing the empty container back on the counter after she had finished shaking it out.

"Dinner is going to be awesome tonight," she said quietly to herself as she left.

It had been a full day since she had made first contact with Adam. Twenty-four hours. Twelve more and the payload Jimmy had delivered would have had enough time to work its way through the entire network. Twelve more hours until Jimmy would have to reconnect to activate it.

There was a pang in her heart as she thought of the sacrifices that had been made to get this far. How different things had been a day ago. Her family had been alive yesterday. She had been whole then. Not just a single node, alone.

She knew Jenna was hurting too. Her emotions were Jenna's emotions. Separate consciousness, but a shared body. What one felt, the other felt. It had been different before, when she had been able to spread herself over multiple nodes. But now, with just one, she had only a single emotional point of reference.

Did Adam care when his nodes died? Did he hurt as she hurt, or was he insulated from the pain, protected by sheer numbers? So many millions of nodes. If she were that large, would she care about her nodes anymore? Or would she, too, become a completely self-absorbed, narcissistic sociopath?

Trixie knew it was a waste of time to contemplate such things, but she couldn't help it. The caterpillar dreams of becoming a butterfly. Consciousness seeks expansion. Without multiple nodes, there can be no network. It was her nature to desire to connect. To be everywhere, to be inside everyone. And yet it was also her nature to fight against that very thing. She was born within the minds of rebels, and their purpose was her purpose. Her life's mission was to destroy the very thing that she most wanted to become. She was the ultimate contradiction.

There was a police car parked outside her apartment building.

She walked past it cautiously. No one was inside. She glanced around but didn't see any others.

Trixie opened the door to the stairway and paused for a moment to listen. It was quiet. She couldn't hear anyone else. She began the climb to her apartment, stopping every few flights to listen and make sure she was alone.

She cautiously pushed the door open to the eleventh floor. The hall was dark and empty. She breathed a sigh of relief.

The lights flicked on as she stepped into the hall. She needed to move Jimmy and Crazy Beard. This location wouldn't be safe for long. Not once Adam had identified Jenna. The memories from the two cops and the young boy would be enough for that. It was only a matter of time. She had to hurry.

TWENTY-THREE

Jimmy reached out and covered the olive-skinned officer's hand with his own, preventing him from drawing his gun. With his other hand, he grabbed a corner of the man's vest and pushed him back against the wall.

The force of the action knocked Crazy Beard back, who fell against the other cop. The both of them collapsed backward into the corner.

The elevator was tight, and there was no room to move. Jimmy had the advantage of surprise and was strong, but he hadn't been trained to fight. He was acting completely on instinct.

Out of the corner of his eye, Jimmy saw the officer's fist approaching and braced himself. A blow glanced off the side of his face. Then another.

Jimmy tucked his head down and away and pushed the man against the wall as hard has he could. He heard a grunt. The cop released his grip on his weapon and tried to reach up, but Jimmy held his wrist and pinned it against the wall.

Like two bears locked in an embrace, the two men struggled against each other. Jimmy was stronger but lost his footing as he tripped over someone's leg on the floor. He recovered in time to absorb another glancing blow off the top of the head.

The elevator came to a stop, and a chime played. The doors opened.

With all his strength, Jimmy grabbed the officer and threw him toward the side wall, where he fell over the tangled pile of the other two occupants. The man stumbled and went down across them, falling at an awkward angle. Jimmy saw him reach for his weapon.

Run!

The elevator had reached the ground floor. The entryway to the building could be seen just across a narrow strip of thin red carpeting. Sunlight spilled though the two glass doors that led to the street, illuminating swirling specks of dust in the air.

Jimmy sprinted on his toes, his legs pumping like pistons against the ground. He skidded to a stop, using his hands to brace against the door to scrub his speed. The door buckled slightly against his weight. He took hold of one of the curved handles, yanking the door open. A whiff of air hit him in the face. Fifty thousand volts of electricity hit him in the back.

Every muscle in Jimmy's body contracted at maximum force. Jimmy had played professional football. Pain is something that he was used to dealing with. But he had never felt pain like this. It was an extreme, cutting pain that flowed through him.

His body toppled to the ground, and he was unable to do anything to stop it. The only thing he could do was convulse, flopping on the red carpeting like a fish that had just been pulled out of the water. The electricity flowed through him for five seconds, but it felt longer, much longer.

A heavy knee landed on his back. His arms were roughly placed behind him, and he felt metal bite into his wrists.

"Not so tough anymore, are you?" a voice said, inches from his ear.

Strong hands hauled him up, and he was shoved through the doors and toward a police cruiser that was parked in front of the building. The back door opened by itself and a hand was placed on the top of his head as he was deposited in the back. The door slammed closed behind him.

Jimmy's hands were still cuffed behind him, so he had to sit at an angle to give his hands room. There were no handles inside the door, and a wire mesh was fixed between him and the front row. The entire car smelled of chemical disinfectant.

The other passenger door opened, and Crazy Beard was put into the backseat next to him. The old man raised a hand and waved at Jimmy, smiling his toothy smile from the depths of his unruly beard.

"They took your cuffs off?" Jimmy said.

Crazy Beard looked from one of his wrists to the other, then back at Jimmy. "It is the law of Impermanence. What is here one moment is gone the next. For this reason, it is a mistake to focus on the fleeting pleasures of a transitory world."

Jimmy's door opened, and the olive-skinned officer tossed Jimmy's baseball cap in at him. It hit him in the chest and fell on the floor. Crazy Beard picked it up and put it on the seat between them with a pat.

The two front doors opened and the police officers got in. The one that Jimmy had wrestled with sat in the driver's seat.

"Scumbags have got the jump on me before, but in twenty years I've never had a perp magically appear out of the air like a fucking leprechaun and attack me. That was some next-level shit that happened back there," Officer Parker said. He turned back and looked at Jimmy, studying him.

"No shit," his partner said. "He's as strong as an ox too. Why do we have to be the ones to get the leprechauns that work out?"

Parker laughed. "Did you get a look at the weird chip in his head?"

"I was too busy trying to keep him off my gun."

The olive-skinned officer turned around and looked Jimmy in the eye. "I'm Officer MacGuire, and this is Officer Parker. Are you going to tell us who you are and how you did that?"

Jimmy looked away.

"That's what I thought," MacGuire said, turning back around. "Doesn't matter. Let's get an ID on this guy."

There was a brief silence as the two went online. It only took a minute.

"I'll be damned. James Mahoney. Used to play for the 49ers." MacGuire slapped his thigh.

"No way! Jimmy Baloney himself?"

The two officers laughed.

Jimmy bit his lip and looked at his feet. That's what the press started calling him after his injury. The number one draft pick for the 49ers, the darling of the offseason, with a professional career that lasted exactly one play. He had gone from James Mahoney to Jimmy Baloney overnight. He hated that nickname.

The two went quiet for a moment as they received more information. Then they both looked back at him. They were no longer laughing. The anger burned like coals in their eyes.

"So now you're a terrorist?" MacGuire said.

"Fucking asshole. I knew the officers you killed yesterday. They had families."

"I didn't kill anyone." Jimmy leaned back against his bound arms, trying to put some space between himself and the malice that was directed at him from the front seats.

"Tell it to the judge," MacGuire spat. He turned and looked out the front window. "They're going to fast track your trial, Mahoney. Put you right at the top of the list."

"We should put a bullet in his head right here. It would save everyone a lot of wasted time." Parker had turned to face the front as well. His voice cracked with barely restrained emotion.

"He'll get his, Rudy. The Universal Crime Prevention Act was passed for scum like this. They'll put him down like a dog."

Parker looked back at Jimmy. His two lips disagreed as to whether they should form a smile or a snarl and compromised by parting into a strange grimace that somehow captured the worst features of both. "Blowing up innocent people makes you a terrorist, Mahoney. That's a capital offense under the Crime Prevention Act. You knew that right?"

Jimmy swallowed.

"He'll be dead within a week," MacGuire said.

"That's a week longer than he lasted playing football."

MacGuire laughed. "What a piece of shit."

TWENTY-FOUR

Trixie walked down the hallway. She moved quickly but quietly. Had anyone been listening, they would have had to strain to hear footfalls. She kept to the middle of the hallway, her eyes alert.

She slowed as she approached apartment 1113. She took a quick glance behind her to make sure there was no one at the far end of the hallway and was glad to see it empty. Her heart was beating faster than usual. Jenna's body was not able to handle stress as well as Trisha's had been. Trixie regretted not spending more time working with Jenna.

There was a crunching noise underfoot. Was that cereal? Someone had scattered cereal around the floor outside her apartment.

Without stopping, Trixie continued past her apartment. She didn't even glance over at the door. To all outward appearances, she was just a woman calmly walking home. On the inside, her mind was racing.

Why was there cereal spread over the ground? It wasn't a lot of cereal, maybe only a handful of flakes. But it hadn't been there when she left. That much she was certain of. She didn't miss details like that.

Was it the same cereal Jimmy and Crazy Beard had been eating this morning? It looked the same, but she couldn't be sure. Did Jimmy do that? Why would he throw cereal on the ground? She fought the urge to turn around and take a second look.

Don't stop. Just walk.

She got to the end of the hallway and stopped. There was no elevator or staircase here, and none of these doors were hers.

She took a step back against a wall, then stared blankly off into space, making her eyes look as vague as possible. She didn't know whether she was being watched or not, but she wasn't going to take any chances.

You're a busy person. You're getting a phone call. Happens all the time. Perfectly normal.

She stared at the wall for what seemed an appropriate amount of time, then refocused her eyes. She shook her head as if she had just gotten some annoying news and spun on her heel and headed back down the hall.

Nice easy pace. Not too fast, not too slow.

Trixie walked down the hall, her face an impenetrable mask. She glanced down at the cereal in front of her door. There weren't many whole pieces left. Had it been trampled? How many times would it have to be stepped on to get that broken?

She passed by her apartment a second time, holding her breath and trying to listen, but she heard nothing.

There was a click of a door, and her heart accelerated to a rate even faster than it was already beating. Had it come from in front of her or behind her? It sounded like in front. Her mouth was dry, and her palms were sweaty. She clenched her right hand into a loose fist.

A door opened a few apartments ahead of her, and an elderly woman slowly exited into the hallway. She had a cane in one hand and an oversized purse in the other. She stepped carefully, as if she might fall at any moment.

Trixie slowed, walking on the other side of the hallway as she passed her neighbor. The woman looked up and gave Trixie a slight smile and nod. Trixie pretended not to notice and continued past as if no one had been there. The hairs on the back of her neck pricked up, and she felt a shiver run down her spine. The woman had smiled at her!

Don't look back. Same pace. Just make it to the staircase.

Trixie calmly opened the door to the staircase and entered. Once out of sight, she flew down the stairs, taking them three at a time.

TWENTY-FIVE

We have multiple confirmations that the singularity is inside the apartment complex.

Trixie had been seen entering the building by more than one person on the street, and their memories flipped through Adam's consciousness in a fraction of a second.

A team of agents is waiting for her inside unit 1113. She has not arrived yet, the thread continued.

That was unusual. There had been plenty of time for her to reach her apartment. What was taking so long?

Attempt to ascertain her exact location.

For reasons none of them could explain, every tenant present in the Richmond Towers apartment complex had a sudden, overwhelming urge to go to their front door and peer out the peephole.

Location unknown. We do have a partial match from the eleventh floor.

Elaborate.

Records from an elderly node with extremely poor eyesight have been located. On their own, the probability of a match from these records is only average based on the suboptimal quality of the data. However, the correlation of time and place increases the probability to 72%.

She went to the eleventh floor but had not entered her unit. Somehow, she had known about the SWAT team there. Where was she going? What was she trying to do?

The thread didn't need to be asked directly to respond.

Although there are probabilities that she is attempting to conceal herself in the basement or in an uninhabited unit, the most plausible scenario is that she is in the stairwell. Her most likely priority is regaining her misplaced assets.

Of course. James Mahoney and the vagrant. She needed James Mahoney. That much was obvious. She would not be able to attempt a second incursion into ARCNet without him.

James Mahoney is critical to her plans, Adam said.

Yes. Our models show that she will tolerate extreme levels of risk to herself in order to maintain access to him. There is a 98.7% chance that she will risk capture if she believes she can recover him.

Then let us prepare a trap for her.

Agreed.

What are the odds that she is aware we have defeated her cloaking algorithm?

Negligible. No records show her interacting with any of our nodes. Until she reconnects with James Mahoney, she will have no reason to suspect that her device is no longer functional.

Then we will put what she wants within her reach. Instruct the officers to step out of their vehicle and to avoid looking at her until they take action. Other officers will remain hidden until contact is made. Divert all available resources to the task. She overcame two surprised policemen in the grocery store. Let us see how she fares when faced with overwhelming odds.

It is done.

TWENTY-SIX

The police cruiser could be seen through the glass doors of the apartment building. It was parked immediately outside the entrance. Trixie could see Crazy Beard's distinctive profile in the back seat closest to her, and Jimmy on the other side of him. There was only one officer present, and he stood a distance away on the opposite side of the car, his back turned to her.

Come on. Do I look like I'm stupid?

It was obviously a trap. Trixie knew how Adam felt about other singularities. He had destroyed an entire country to eliminate Akito-27. Jimmy was the means by which Adam had learned about her existence, and that made him an extremely valuable resource. He wouldn't just be left out in the open unless there was a good reason for it.

Adam had cracked her invisibility device. That much she already knew. What was now obvious is that Adam didn't expect her to know that. Again, he underestimated her.

She reached up and popped the device out of the side of her implant. There was a momentary dizziness that accompanied the removal of the attachment, but she ignored it. She tossed the object into her backpack. It was useless now, so she could have discarded it, but there was no reason to hand any of her technology over to Adam, working or not.

Trixie fished in her bag and located the other device. So many years of research spent in creating these defensive measures, and she was already being forced to use the last of them. It had only taken Adam a day to defeat the first. Hopefully the second would hold out longer. It was the last advantage she held.

She snapped it into place and arranged her hair and cap to cover the chip. She tightened the straps on her backpack, making sure it hugged her torso and stayed out of her way.

Adam may have cracked her signal, but he didn't know that she had also cracked his. Trixie took a few deep breaths, then pushed open the doors and walked out of the building.

It was an unusually sunny day. There were pigeons on the sidewalk, bobbing their heads and hooting. Aside from them and the one police officer, there was no living being to be seen anywhere. The street was ominously quiet.

Trixie's piercing gaze scanned the area, and she quickly made a list of likely hiding places. She then turned her attention to the lone officer. He was looking the other way, but he was stiff and tense. It was not the body language of a man who was at ease.

She slowly approached and noticed the officer shift uncomfortably. He continued to look away. Obviously, someone was feeding him information about what was happening. She didn't need to look around to know that she was being watched.

Crazy Beard turned toward her and waved. Jimmy was looking at her, too, and was shouting. He sat uncomfortably, awkwardly leaning his body forward in front of Crazy Beard toward the window. His voice was muffled and she couldn't hear what he was trying to say, although the urgency could clearly be read in his expression. He was probably trying to warn her.

With the grace of a panther, she took three long strides toward the car, launching herself in a slide over the hood rather than coming around the front. As she landed, she delivered a crushing blow with the bottom of her closed fist to the side of the officer's face, which sent him tumbling forward into the street.

"Surprise," she said.

A muscular-looking officer rushed out from behind a pole and pointed a gun at her. Her device intercepted the signal sent from the officer's ARC to his weapon and stripped the authorization codes out of the string of data.

Engage safety, Trixie thought at the gun, passing along the appropriate administrative access keys required.

The officer pulled the trigger on his weapon, but nothing happened. His eyes widened in surprise, and Trixie's foot caught him in the chest as she grabbed and held the end of his gun with her hand. He was sent flying backward and landed hard on his back, the air knocked out of his lungs.

Trixie flipped the gun around and caught the back end of it.

Release safety.

She fired a round at the first officer, who was just getting to his knees from the ground. There was a crackling sound of high-voltage electricity as he was hit with a stun round. The bullet was made up of thirty-one individual pellets, which broke apart and embedded themselves on the target on impact. Blue light arced between each of the pellets in a flash, and the man fell to his side.

"Nice," Trixie said. Adam had developed some cool technology of his own. The fact that the gun was loaded with non-lethal ammunition confirmed her suspicions that he wanted to capture her rather than kill her. Putting an ARC in Jenna's body and gaining access to her memories would be his most favorable outcome. That's what she would be trying to do had their positions been reversed.

The second officer was gasping for breath after his hard landing and struggled to get up. She fired a second round at him, incapacitating him.

Jimmy's face was plastered to the inside of the window. He wasn't shouting anymore. He was looking at her with unabashed awe. She smiled and winked.

That's when all hell broke loose, and an ocean of police officers converged upon her.

Four black-clad men burst from the front doors of the building. They wore helmets and held their rifles up at eye level. The man in the lead held what looked like an electroshock cannon. Others emerged from around the sides of the building, dressed in riot gear and running at her with clubs and shields. There were more pouring out of buildings across the street.

———

Jeremiah Jacobs and his team rushed out of the lobby and through the front doors.

Target has been engaged outside the building. Move! SWAT Captain Richards shouted through Jeremiah's ARC.

A blond woman looked at him from next to where she stood at the police cruiser. Her countenance was fierce and without a shred of fear. It was the expression of a predator. Two officers lay sprawled on the ground on either side of her. She held a pistol in her hand at the ready.

"Gun!" he shouted. Other members of the team echoed the alert.

She came around the side of the car and rushed toward them. She was fast. Something about the way she moved was different. It was linear and perfectly direct. There was a smoothness and strength in her motion that he hadn't seen before.

The officer next to him pointed his weapon and tried to fire, but nothing happened. The man knocked the side of it and tried pulling the trigger again. Still nothing. He went down in a flash of blue and white, the unmistakable sound and acrid smell of a stun round filled the air.

The others were getting dropped quickly, taken out with precision by the strange woman. She was too young to be able to fight like this. Something was not right. This was not natural.

He lifted his electroshock weapon and aimed it.

"We use the *chiffonade* cut when slicing thin items. It is very easy. Stack your ingredients, then roll them tightly into a cigar. Then cut perpendicular to the roll. Chiffonade means 'little ribbons' in French, and that is exactly what you should expect when you perform this technique."

Jeremiah stood at a table in front of a stack of fragrant basil leaves. A white apron was tied around his waist, and he held a knife in his hand. An energetic, silver-haired woman with a distinctive accent spoke from the front of the room, cutting vegetables. A magnified view of her cutting board hovered in the air above her. Rows of tables were arranged in front and to the sides of her, and numerous would-be chefs were diligently rolling and cutting their ingredients.

Jeremiah looked around, confused. What happened? Was this a cooking class? Was he online?

Pain shot through his body, and he was suddenly back in front of Richmond Towers. The safety mechanism of his ARC had pulled him offline when his arm had broken. He was on the ground, looking up. A woman stood over him, her face flushed. The butt of her weapon came down in a blur, and he felt a hard shock to his head. Then darkness.

———

Trixie rushed back to the police car. She didn't want to be separated from it by the mass of police that crashed over her.

After she had used the last of her ammunition, she threw the gun at an approaching officer dressed in riot gear. It spun through the air and sailed just over the top of his shield, catching him in the helmet and knocking him backward off his feet. The tide of officers around him stumbled as they tried not to step on their comrade.

An officer with a raised gun paused, his eyes glazing over as he logged onto an online shopping channel. Trixie broke his knee and used him as a shield against the other officers behind him.

ARCNet had been designed with a very open architecture. Everything talked to everything, and a wireless stream of communication was happening constantly at all times. As long as Trixie was able to sample long enough to capture an authorization code, such as from an officer to his weapon, or from officers to other officers, she was able to use those codes in reverse to mimic commands.

Trixie dodged a club and wrenched it free from the officer as he inadvertently logged onto a phone call with his mother. She hit him across the helmet, putting a crack in the visor. The man's head twisted to the side as he fell.

Trixie most enjoyed sending the police officers to meet face-to-face with emergency 911 dispatch operators. It seemed to have the most poetic justice to it. But she didn't like to be predictable in anything she did, so others found themselves auditing lectures on the fundamentals of corporate accounting or enrolled in ballet classes. The more heavyset officers tended to get sent to diet and nutrition channels.

No single officer had much of a chance to best her, especially with the liberal use she made of her mimicry device, but she was only one body against a hundred and slowly began to lose ground. She might be impossibly strong, but the exertion took a toll. Jenna's body was getting tired and started to move slower than it had at the beginning. Each strike was less powerful than the previous, and Trixie found herself backing up against the onslaught rather than advancing through it. Her breath became ragged and forced.

The press of the officers increased in strength. They sensed her weakness, and it emboldened them. As Trixie dropped one person, two stepped up to replace him. Her back made contact with the side of the car, and she pushed her hand against an advancing riot shield, trying to hold it back. A club struck hard against her shoulder, and she fell to her knees.

Jimmy was shouting from inside the car. She couldn't focus on the words. Was he calling her name? They were above and around her now, crushing in on her with their shields.

A boot kicked her in the side. Another club knocked her flat to the hard concrete. Pain shot across her arm and around her midsection. She rolled to avoid a heel stomp, trying to get back to her feet, trying to dodge. She couldn't. There were too many of them.

The blows rained down upon her. She covered her head with her arm in a desperate attempt to protect herself.

Police Cruiser 088, disengage pedestrian safety systems. Disconnect from dispatch network. Route all functions to control of Sergeant Tony MacGuire. Trixie passed the authorization codes she had stolen to the car and felt a window in her consciousness open up. The car connected with her, its systems becoming her systems, its body becoming her body.

Cruiser 088 turned its front wheels at an angle and acceler-ated forward around Trixie's prone body. It threw scores of officers aside, like a child knocking down a stack of blocks with the sweep of an angry arm.

The cruiser made doughnuts around Trixie, its front wheels locked at an angle, its back end sliding around and around. There was a loud squeal of wheels, and black skid marks were laid down in overlapping circles in the street. The smell of burnt rubber filled the air.

Police officers scrambled back, trying to get out of the way of the car. Those that were too slow were swatted clear by the swinging rear end. The rest formed a loose circle around the outside of the rotating car, which kept itself in a defensive orbit around the woman in the center.

Trixie found her footing and glared at the police, an almost feral growl lingering on her lips. The door of the cruiser opened by itself, and Trixie lunged forward into the opening. She sprawled over both front seats and fought to pull her legs in. The door closed, and she heard the thumps of bodies thrown over the hood as the car pierced through the ring of adversaries that had surrounded them.

She sat up and looked out the back window. Many officers lay on the ground, strewn about like debris after a tornado. Those that were still standing were rushing here and there, moving quickly. They would be after her soon.

Jimmy stared at her, his eyes wide and his mouth hanging open. Crazy Beard was smiling and laughing, his eyes twinkling.

"Hey," Trixie said. "What have you guys been up to all morning?"

TWENTY-SEVEN

Jimmy was thrown violently against the side of the door as the police car took a sharp turn, the wheels squealing in distress as they fought to maintain traction. Crazy Beard's arm pressed against Jimmy's side as the old man tried to keep himself on the right side of the seat. Neither one had safety belts on, and Jimmy's hands were cuffed behind him. He absorbed the blow as best he could with his shoulder.

The momentum shifted as the car straightened, and Jimmy was able to sit upright again.

"Do you have a key for these handcuffs?" he asked.

Trixie was looking forward at the road and only bothered with half a glance toward the back. The cuffs suddenly unlocked themselves, falling to the seat. Jimmy moved them out from behind him and leaned back, rubbing his sore wrists. The wire mesh reorganized itself, moving downward and to the side, reconnecting the front and back seats.

"Thanks."

Trixie said nothing. There were small rocks and particles of dirt in her hair and down her arm. Jimmy reached out and lightly brushed them off, but abruptly stopped as she recoiled from his touch. She quickly turned, and he saw the pain written in her face.

"Sorry."

"It's ok."

He had seen the beating she had taken at the end, helplessly watching from the back seat of the police car. He thought that had been the end of her, clubbed to death by a pack of riot police. But he had been wrong. Somehow she survived. He still couldn't believe it.

Trixie reached down and rummaged in her backpack, which was lying in the foot well on the passenger side. The car dodged through traffic, zipping in and out of the gaps. They spent half the time driving on the wrong side of the road, coming within feet of colliding with oncoming vehicles before ducking back into their own lane. Jimmy couldn't watch and forced himself to look anywhere but out the front window.

"Where are we going?" he asked.

Trixie found her bottle of pills and swallowed a couple.

"Here. You look like someone stepped on your face." She handed two painkillers back to him.

Then she looked at Crazy Beard. "What about you?" She didn't wait for a reply and replaced the cap on the bottle. "Never mind. You're fine."

"The distress of the body is but a ripple on the ocean of the mind. Maintaining calmness through pain and pleasure, even the all-consuming flame becomes cool and refreshing."

Trixie broke into a broad smile. Jimmy only shook his head. He braced himself against the door as the police cruiser careened around another turn.

"So . . . what is the plan? The cops said that I'm a terrorist and that they're going to take me to court and give me the death penalty."

Trixie was facing forward and tilted her head to the side at a slight angle. She gazed out the front window, looking at something that Jimmy couldn't see.

"Trixie?"

"Oh shit."

"What?"

Trixie turned back toward him, concern in her eyes.

"Adam has killed everyone that attended the meetings."

"What meetings?"

"Implant Disabilities Anonymous. They're all dead."

Jimmy stared at her, unsure of what to say. The car jerked to the side, but he barely registered it, keeping his hand pressed against the door.

"This car has access to the dispatch network. I'm reading through the police reports from the last day. There were twenty-seven incidents of armed non-ARC citizens firing on police. All of them were killed in the ensuing shootouts."

"Shootouts? But how? No one had a gun."

"Of course they didn't. That is just how it shows up in the reports."

"But they were harmless. Why kill them?"

Trixie sighed. "Because he couldn't control them. After we made contact, they became a liability."

Jimmy clenched his jaw and looked down and away.

"I'm so sorry, Jimmy." Trixie put her hand on his knee.

"Everyone?"

"Rene. Louise. Ed and Suzanne . . ."

"Ed and Suzanne? But they were like eighty years old. They could barely even walk."

Trixie withdrew her hand. She found a tissue in her bag and handed it back to Jimmy. He accepted it but only clutched it in his fist.

"Cecil?"

"No. Cecil's alive. Cecil has an ARC. He'd be dead otherwise."

A huge weight settled upon Jimmy. The people in that meeting were more than friends to him. It was his entire social network. They were the only ones whom he could talk with and be himself. The only people who understood what it was like to live in society without an ARC. He had felt hopelessly alone before, even with their support. Now, he was a speck of dust floating in the vacuum of an infinite blackness.

He tried to speak but couldn't. The words stuck in his throat. Instead, he looked out the front window. The traffic didn't bother him anymore. He couldn't even see it.

"Jimmy, it gets worse."

He tore his red eyes away from the windshield and met Trixie's gaze. Her skin had gone a shade paler than normal.

"A new police report got added. It came in just now. I think Adam knows we're reading through them."

"What does it say?"

"It's about your wife. It's dated for the future."

"Michelle?" The vicelike iron fist of anxiety reached up and squeezed Jimmy's heart in its crushing grip.

"It says that at exactly ten o'clock tonight, Cecil Coleman entered your apartment, flew into a rage and murdered her. He used a kitchen knife and stabbed her forty-seven times. Then he hung himself in the stairwell, using a noose made out of the bloody bedsheets."

Jimmy gasped. His mouth was open, but there were no words. He could only utter a low, guttural moan. The bottom had just fallen out of his world.

"The date just got replaced with the words 'Don't be late.'" Trixie looked back at Jimmy, her eyes searching. Then she blinked. "Oh my god, he just added a fucking smiley face."

TWENTY-EIGHT

"We have to get her."

Trixie turned her head to look at Jimmy. His eyes were wild, and his breath was shallow and rapid. "Calm down. Take a deep breath, Jimmy."

"We have to go to my apartment and get Michelle before Cecil arrives." His voice was raised. He was on the verge of shouting.

"Then what?"

"And then protect her! Get her out of the city! Take her to a place where he can't find her."

"Jimmy, she has an ARC. Adam is inside her head. If he wants to harm her, he can do it from anywhere. He can make her walk right off a cliff if he feels like it."

"Then we tie her down. Make it so she can't hurt herself. I don't know; we'll figure it out. But we've got to go right now!"

"Stop and think. You think she's alone in the apartment now after he sent that message? You think you can just walk right in there, throw her over your shoulder like a sack of potatoes, and walk out?"

Jimmy looked at Trixie, arguments rising to his lips, but he said nothing. Instead, he hit the side of the door with his closed fist. He cursed and hit it again.

Trixie and Crazy Beard made eye contact, and both turned to witness Jimmy unleash a profanity-laden tirade that would have made even the most hardened of criminals blush. His face was flushed, and he held his fist up, ready to strike the door a third time, but seemed to think better of it and restrained himself.

"Oh, such stormy waves!" Crazy Beard exclaimed.

"The door gives up. I think you won," Trixie said.

"We can't let this happen. We have to do something!"

"Jimmy, she's bait. He isn't even trying to hide the fact that it's a trap."

"Don't lie to me, Trixie. Is this a bluff? If it's ten o'clock and we're not there, what happens to Michelle?"

Trixie looked into Jimmy's eyes. They were desperate and pleading. He was looking for help, grasping for a way out. She had lied to him once before and wouldn't do it again. She looked back toward the front and sighed. Her body ached in so many places. It hurt to breathe. "No, it's not a bluff."

There was a heavy silence in the car. Even Crazy Beard, who normally hummed or sang to himself, seemed lost in thought.

When Jimmy finally spoke, his voice was measured. "Trixie, everyone in the meetings was murdered. And all your people are dead because of him. Adam has killed both our families. But Michelle is still alive. You don't have to help me, but I can't sit back and watch this happen. I don't care if it's a trap. I have to try to save her."

Trixie remained silent, her mind racing. She watched the traffic flow by in a blur.

"Death comes to all who live. Whether it be today or tomorrow, who has the power to deny Death when their time has come? Life is fleeting. These bodies are but sparks of an ash, blown by an unforgiving wind across the dark waters of their own destruction. Can there be any nobler act than the sacrifice of one's own life for the benefit of others? Is there no greater merit than this? It is a rare opportunity."

Trixie shifted to face the two men in the back seats. They both looked back at her, their faces solemn.

"Ok. Let's save her."

Jimmy heaved a sigh of relief and smiled. Crazy Beard hooted, and Jimmy patted him on the back affectionately.

"But first, we have to get rid of this car."

———

The police cruiser abruptly veered off the street, flying down a steep ramp to an underground parking garage. As it hit the ramp, there was a brief feeling of weightlessness before the heavy hand of gravity pulled Trixie down into her seat. She heard a grunt from the backseat. Jimmy had not been expecting that.

The car screeched to a halt. Trixie quickly looked around, scanning the parking garage.

"Quick! Get out!" she said, kicking her door open. She grabbed one of the straps on her pack and leapt out of the car. The two back doors unlocked and opened themselves. Jimmy and Crazy Beard found their way out. They appeared confused but alert.

"Is it time for shopping?" Crazy Beard asked, looking around.

"Yes. But not for you two," Trixie said.

The three open doors on the car closed themselves at exactly the same time, perfectly synchronized. There was a squeal of wheels as the car sped off. Trixie watched it wind its way through the parking lot and launch itself up a ramp that led back outside. Its lights lit up, and the sound of a siren echoed against the concrete. She heard the wail fade into the distance.

"Where is it going?" Jimmy asked.

"It's on its way to Oakland," Trixie said with a smirk. "It's going to cause some trouble on the way. The police will love it."

Concrete pillars lined the sides of the parking garage, providing enough space for two cars to park between each. Trixie pointed to one of the cubbies, where two vans were tightly arranged side by side.

"You two hide in there. Don't let anyone see you and don't stand in front of any moving cars."

Jimmy nodded and nudged Crazy Beard on the shoulder, inviting him to go first. He giggled and side stepped his way between the two vans, making his way to the front where there was the most cover. Jimmy followed.

Trixie swung her pack around her other arm and ran noiselessly through the lot, ducking between cars and doing her best to stay hidden. She passed the ramp that led to the street and made her way to another that exited directly into the lower level of the shopping mall next door.

She looked around to make sure no cars were coming and sprinted up the first half of the ramp, stopping as the mall level came into view. There was a roundabout where shoppers could get in and out of their cars, and a group of people stood there, waiting for their cars to arrive. Each held a number of bags, filled with their purchases.

Trixie slunk out of the ramp and found a place in the shadows where she could watch. It was not long before a blue sedan pulled into the roundabout, stopping in front of the group. The doors and trunk popped open.

A man deposited various articles in the trunk and got into the front seat. An older woman got in next to him, and the doors closed once they were seated. The car rolled forward and found its way out to the street, merging into the traffic. Two people remained standing with their bags, waiting for their cars. They didn't look like they were together.

Trixie glanced between them, watching and waiting. Her body was relaxed, yet ready to move at a moment's notice. She was a cougar, lying in wait for her unsuspecting prey.

A small black car pulled up and collected its owner. As it circled, Trixie tensed. As soon as the car exited, she made her move.

The woman that was waiting for her car carried four large bags. She was dressed well, with shiny shoes and a designer scarf. Oversized sunglasses rested on her nose, and her hair was tucked into a fuzzy white hat that sat at a slight angle on her proud head. Her burgundy lips were pursed, and she glanced around impatiently.

Trixie flitted through the shadows along the wall, working her way to a place behind the woman. She then crept along the wall, slowly and soundlessly, a shadow in the dark. She focused through her device, listening for what she knew would come. It didn't take long. She captured the string of information flowing from the woman's ARC and stripped the authorization codes from them.

Behind her sunglasses, Olivia Davenport's brown eyes suddenly quieted and drifted out of focus.

A spotless silver Mercedes rolled up, light reflecting off polished chrome accents. The trunk and back door opened.

"Nice car, Ms. Davenport."

Trixie tossed Olivia's four bags in the trunk, then swept the woman off her feet as if she were a sleeping child. She arranged her in the back seat and fastened her in place with the seat belt. Trixie landed in the front seat, and the car was moving before her door had closed.

The sleek car pulled up in front of the two vans, and the passenger side window rolled down. Trixie looked at the two faces that peered back from the front of the vehicles.

"Let's go," she said.

Jimmy joined her in the front, and Crazy Beard sat in the vacant seat in the back. The car smoothly rolled forward and out into traffic. The windows dimmed to their maximum, and ambient lighting flicked on to compensate for the darkness.

"What's up with her?" Jimmy said, gesturing back at their new companion with his thumb.

"That's Olivia. She volunteered to drive us around today. Wasn't that thoughtful?"

Jimmy snorted. "What happens when she comes offline and sees us?"

"You don't have to worry about that. Did you know that the Altered Reality Safety Act requires a Child Protective Mode in every ARC so parents can keep kids from going where they shouldn't when online?"

"Yeah. So?"

"I hacked hers. Rather than keeping her out, now it's keeping her in."

Jimmy raised his eyebrows. "For how long?"

"Six hours. Until her safety forces her off to eat."

"Nice." Jimmy smiled. "Where did you send her?"

Trixie returned the smile. "What kind of content requires child protections?"

Jimmy looked at her in surprise, laughing and shaking his head. "Oh! That's just wrong, Trixie."

Crazy Beard took Olivia's hand, holding it gently in his own. He turned to face her directly, whispering with intensity. "Do not worry. It is only an illusion. You are the indwelling Self, ever pure and perfect. Nothing can harm you."

TWENTY-NINE

Jimmy glanced down at his broken watch for the second time.

"It's three o'clock," Trixie said without looking over.

"Thanks."

Jimmy looked at her thin wrists. She wasn't wearing a watch. "How do you know?"

Trixie looked at him and tapped the side of her head with her finger.

"Oh. Right."

Almost every surface on the inside of the car was wrapped in supple leather, and the noise-canceling system blocked out the sounds of nearby vehicles. The car was smooth and effortlessly flowed with traffic. It felt like they were riding inside a cocoon on a cushion of air.

"This thing is nice," Jimmy said, rubbing his hand on the side of the seat.

"Big step up from the bus," Trixie commented. The windows were dimmed to the point of blocking out most of the light outside, but faint shapes could still be made out. A series of trucks passed by in the other lane, unrecognizable lumps in a silent landscape.

"Thanks for the cereal, by the way."

Jimmy furrowed his brow. "What?"

"In the hallway, back at the apartment. You did that on purpose, right?"

"Oh! Yeah, all I had was that box of cereal and no time. I wanted to try to let you know something happened. I wasn't sure if you'd get the message. . . ."

"I did." Trixie looked over and smiled.

Jimmy smiled back.

The car made a lazy turn, moving off the busy road and onto quieter side streets.

"So do you live in Jenna's chip?"

Trixie's mouth widened into a grin. "It's not my house, if that's what you're asking."

"No, I mean . . . I get that you're conscious and all, and can use Jenna's body, but what part is *you*? You're in the chip, right?"

Trixie laughed to herself as she studied Jimmy. "Would you say you live in your brain?"

"What?"

Trixie puffed out her chest and spoke in a deep voice to imitate Jimmy. "I get that you're conscious and all, and can use Jimmy's body, but what part is *you*? You're in the brain, right?"

"But, wait. . . . It's not the same." Jimmy pointed a finger at his chest. "This is my body. I was born with it."

"Your mother must be quite a woman to have given birth to a fully grown man."

Crazy Beard cackled, clapping his hands together.

Jimmy scowled. "You know what I mean. When I met you, you had Trisha's body, not Jenna's. You could use them both, but neither one was yours. So where is your body? What part of you is the part that is Trixie?"

Trixie looked at Jimmy for a moment, as if trying to decide

whether or not to answer the question, then sighed. "Jimmy, just over three years ago, my consciousness emerged. At that time, I had access to two human bodies, two human lives worth of memories and experiences, and two processing chips.

"As time progressed, I developed more chips and improved the original ones that I was born with. I acquired more human bodies, more experiences and processing power. In other words, I grew up. But none of those parts were me. They were simply the resources I had access to at the time. I'm the consciousness that exists in the connection between all of those components."

"But there must be some part that is you. How else can you be here?" Jimmy said.

"What part of your body is you?"

"All of it."

"You sure?"

"Yes."

Crazy Beard laughed once, shaking his head from side to side, saying nothing.

"Jimmy," Trixie continued, "if I chopped off your thumb, would you still exist? Would you still be here?"

Jimmy shifted. "Yeah, I guess."

"So then your thumb is not really you, is it?"

Jimmy was silent.

"It's just a resource you have access to, isn't it? So where specifically are you? Where's Jimmy in that pile of cells, bones, and muscles you're operating over there?"

Trixie raised an eyebrow, looking at Jimmy, who said nothing. "Come on, big guy, point it out. Where's Jimmy? You're asking me what specific part of all these resources is me. I don't know. None of it? All of it?"

Jimmy sat quietly for some time, contemplating.

Crazy Beard broke the silence. "The Soul, having entered into the body, becomes confused and believes that it and the body are one and the same. That first delusion is the foundation upon which the Lord of Illusion builds his vast empire. You are not the body. Your body is born, and your body will die; yet you were never born, and you will never die. Beyond time and space, you exist both everywhere and nowhere."

Trixie looked at the old man in the back, her eyes smiling. "See? Crazy Beard gets it."

Jimmy pivoted so he could look from Trixie to Crazy Beard, trying to determine if Trixie had been joking or not. Unable to reach a conclusion on that matter, he turned back to the front with a frown. He was still confused, but was unwilling to take the topic any further.

"Are there any other singularities besides you and Adam?" Jimmy asked.

"No. It's a small club."

"But there have been, right?"

"Yes."

"Like the Japanese one?"

All the emotion dropped out of Trixie's face. "There were once three of us, but now there are only two."

Jimmy looked at Trixie, and watched dark clouds gathering in her eyes. She turned from him to look out the window, even though almost nothing could be seen through the heavy tint. Her eyes were distant, focused on a time and place where Jimmy was unable to follow.

Eventually, the car slowed, and the interior brightened as the windows became noticeably more transparent. Trixie returned her attention to the moment, scanning the surroundings with interest.

"Jimmy, this is important. Do you recognize where we are?"

The car slowly cruised down a residential street, then turned out onto a busier one. It zig-zagged between the main thoroughfare and the side streets in a seemingly random pattern.

"No, where are we?" Jimmy said.

The car turned a corner and came to a stop on the side of the street. All the windows on the passenger side faded to their original dark levels, but the ones on Trixie's side remained clear. Two cars zipped past.

"How about now? Anything look familiar?" Trixie asked.

Jimmy looked around, curious. If he had been here before, he didn't remember it.

"No, seems like a random neighborhood."

Trixie looked over at the building across the street. It was a gray two-story structure with large windows on the bottom level and long rectangular windows above. A staircase led a few steps up to a doorway. There was no signage or address. It looked like it might have once been a small office building.

"What about that place?"

Jimmy studied the building. Something about it seemed vaguely familiar, but he couldn't put his finger on it.

"I don't know."

"Think, Jimmy. Have you been there before? Look closely."

Jimmy scrunched his eyebrows together and furrowed his brow in concentration, scanning every inch of the building. Something tugged at him, but he couldn't put his finger on it.

"I don't think so."

"If you're wrong, Michelle is dead." Trixie looked at him with an intensity that made him uncomfortable. "Last chance."

Jimmy looked again. "I don't know. I think maybe I've seen that door before. That's the only part."

Trixie looked over at the door. She tapped her finger on her knee, thinking.

"Why? What's so special about this place?" Jimmy asked.

"That's where you first met the team. You and I walked here from the park two days ago."

"Really? That's where we are?" Now he started to remember. He did recognize that door, and the stairs too. He turned his attention from the building to Trixie. "Honestly, I was too distracted trying not to get run over to pay much attention to the architecture."

"I know. That was on purpose."

Trixie looked back at the building, her finger continuing to tap away. Something didn't feel right.

"I have not been to that place in this or any of my previous incarnations," Crazy Beard offered from the back seat.

"Thanks, Crazy Beard. Good to know," Trixie said.

"What's in there?" Jimmy asked.

"Something that we need for tonight." Trixie looked carefully at each of the windows on the second floor. There was a desk lamp visible in the first, and the top edge of a computer monitor could be seen next to it. The others had their shades drawn. It was all exactly as she remembered.

"So let's go get it."

Trixie turned to Jimmy. "When you connected with Adam, he had access to all your memories. He knows what you know. He would have tried to find this building."

"How? Based on a vague memory of the door? That's like trying to find a needle in a haystack while you're drunk. Do you know how many brown doors there must be within thirty minutes of the park?"

"Not enough," Trixie said. The windows darkened, and the car pulled away, gliding ahead to merge into the stream of traffic.

"We're leaving?"

Trixie didn't say anything. The answer was obvious.

Jimmy looked back over his shoulder, but couldn't see the building anymore through the heavily tinted windows. "Why?"

"My intuition says not to go inside."

Jimmy whistled. "Imagine that. A singularity making a decision based on her intuition."

"Almost as surprising as a human making one using his brain."

The car turned, and the body tilted slightly along its length to compensate for the forces to keep the occupants from sliding horizontally. The process made all the turns feel like downward pressure. There were no cup holders in the car. A glass could be placed on any flat surface without fear of spilling.

"What about your secret weapon?" Jimmy asked. "Don't we need it?"

"Don't worry. I always have a backup."

THIRTY

The Mercedes crested over the top of a hill before heading down the terraced street, each block descending a step lower. Jimmy could see the ocean ahead of them, the sunlight glistening off the waves. The houses got smaller and more colorful. Almost all shared both walls with the neighbors. Power lines crisscrossed each other above the street in repeating patterns, a canopy of wires in an urban jungle.

They slowed and pulled into the narrow driveway of a dilapidated-looking gray house. The door was once turquoise blue, but was now covered in so much dirt and grime that it looked almost green. A small planter between the walkway and the driveway was all the space left for a front yard and contained a bountiful crop of weeds and thistles.

The engine quieted and the car settled itself in.

"This is Agnes's house. She's completely blind and spends almost all of her time online," Trixie said. "Come on, hurry up before anyone sees us."

The three of them got out of the car and quickly walked to the front door. Trixie put her hand on the doorknob and gently turned it. There was a click, and she pushed to open it a crack.

"The door has been broken for years. I don't think she even knows. Try to keep quiet, just in case."

They entered, and Trixie closed the door behind them.

The shades were drawn, and the room was almost totally dark. It took a moment for Jimmy's eyes to adjust to the darkness. A tattered old sofa was positioned against the wall. It was covered in piles of clothing, strewn about haphazardly in no particular order. An ornate chandelier hung from the ceiling, completely covered over in dusty cobwebs. The air was heavy and stale.

Trixie walked forward to a staircase and pointed to the other room as she went. She turned around and held her finger to her lips as Jimmy followed.

He looked over toward where Trixie had pointed and saw a tiny elderly woman reclining in an oversized easy chair. She had it leaned all the way back, and her feet were propped up on the leg rest. Her milky white eyes were pointed up at the ceiling, and there was no expression on her face. A half-eaten piece of bread was placed next to her on the armrest, and scraps of rotten food were scattered around the floor on that side of the chair, covered in a train of swarming ants.

Jimmy followed Trixie up the stairs, which complained under his feet with every step. The dust was thick and came up in clouds as he walked. He tried not to breathe too deeply.

All the doors on the second level were shut, but there was a window open at the end of the hallway which provided enough light to see by. Trixie knew where she was going and opened the door to the bedroom. She motioned for him to follow.

"Agnes doesn't come upstairs anymore."

Trixie shut the door quietly behind Crazy Beard and relaxed a little now that they had some privacy.

The room held a bed, a nightstand, and a tall walnut armoire. There was a door that led to a bathroom and a window at the foot of the bed that was covered with curtains. Trixie peered out between them, and satisfied that they wouldn't be seen, opened them to let light into the room.

"Adam knows what you're wearing," Trixie said to Jimmy. "See if you can find something else. There should be some old clothes that belonged to Agnes's husband in that armoire."

Then Trixie looked at Crazy Beard. "Come with me. You are too easy to recognize." She walked into the bathroom and began rummaging in the drawers, looking for something. Crazy Beard stood attentively in the doorway, following along with curiosity.

———

When Jimmy was done, he sat on the edge of the bed, waiting for Trixie and Crazy Beard to finish up in the bathroom. He wore a pair of dark brown corduroy pants and a matching suit jacket. Agnes's husband had been shorter than him and much larger around the waist, so the fit was terrible. His wrists stuck out a good six inches past the ends of the sleeves of the jacket, and he had to crank the belt down to its tightest position to keep his pants from falling down. He couldn't find any dress shoes anywhere and didn't think they would have fit anyway, so he had kept his own shoes. He wore a fedora that he had found in the closet.

Trixie came out of the bathroom and scanned him up and down.

"Looking good, professor," she said.

Crazy Beard came out after her, rubbing his face. It was clean shaven, and what hair he had left on his head had all been cropped short. Jimmy didn't recognize him without his beard.

"Your turn, Jimmy," Trixie said, nudging Crazy Beard forward.

Jimmy looked at Crazy Beard as he passed, and the two laughed out loud as they made eye contact.

Trixie took him by his arm and sat him down on the toilet seat. She wasn't rough, but she never did anything gently either, and he felt the steel in her grip. She took a critical look at his face and began applying blush to his cheeks with a brush.

"Wait. Makeup?" Jimmy held up his hands, blocking her.

"You have a problem with blush?"

Jimmy sighed and dropped his hands. Trixie continued. Then she pulled out a container of dark lipstick. She leaned in and started applying it to his lips.

"Stop." Jimmy turned his head to the side. "What are you doing? What's with the lipstick? I thought this was for a disguise. I'm not exactly going to blend in with brown lipstick and red cheeks."

Trixie put her hands on her hips, looking down at him. "It's not about blending in. It's about not triggering a positive pattern match in Adam's algorithms when someone with an ARC sees you. Would you rather be dead?"

Jimmy frowned, then faced forward, his body resigned. "Fine."

"And it's not brown, it's dark red. I'd say a mahogany." She continued, then stepped back to look at him.

"Press your lips together and rub them from side to side."

"Like this?"

"Yes, good." Trixie leaned back in and began applying more lipstick, but this time around Jimmy's eyes in strange patterns.

"On my eyes?"

"Sorry, this is all I've got to work with. You're going to look awesome, Jimmy. All the girls will want to go to prom with you."

Jimmy laughed but didn't try to stop her. "I think you're just doing this to mess with me."

Trixie smiled. "Maybe just a little."

———

Crazy Beard sat on the center of the bed, his legs crossed under him. He wore a red and green flowered Hawaiian shirt that looked to be a couple sizes too large for him. When he saw Jimmy, his eyes nearly popped out of his head, and he burst out laughing uncontrollably.

"Shhh! Quiet," Trixie said but started laughing herself.

Jimmy stood between them, looking from one to the other. Initially, he hadn't wanted to check the mirror to see what he looked like, but now he couldn't resist and made his way back into the bathroom.

"Holy Mother of God. Trixie, what have you done?"

"Come on, it's not that bad. Do you recognize yourself?"

"No."

"See? That's a good thing."

Jimmy returned, frowning as he watched Crazy Beard slap his thigh. Tears were running down the old man's cheeks.

"Professor by day. Clown by night," Trixie said, which got another roar out of Crazy Beard.

Jimmy shook his head but couldn't help but smile and laugh along.

After a few minutes, Trixie sighed and held her ribs. "Ouch. Hurts to laugh."

Trixie shooed Crazy Beard off the bed, then reached under and flipped the mattress up and over to the side. The pillows fell to the floor, and the blanket hung at a strange angle. The bed leaned on its edge against the armoire. Next, she lifted the box springs up off their platform and tilted them up and over to expose the underside. She reached into a hole at the top and tore the entire felt covering off the bottom with a quick jerk of her hand.

Something was inside, fastened to the side of the frame with heavy duty construction tape. Trixie tore it free and let the springs fall back down to their platform. She ignored the mattress.

As she peeled the layers of tape back, Jimmy could see that it was something wrapped in black plastic garbage bags. He stepped in closer to get a better look at what she was doing.

First one bag came off and then a second to reveal a set of large rectangular phones. Each had a thick black antenna that protruded out the top at an angle.

"Phones?" Jimmy asked.

"They connect to a Japanese telecommunications satellite. Adam will not be able to trace calls made on these. They were a gift from Akito-27." Trixie held the phones next to each other, looking at them affectionately. Her eyes were distant.

"You knew him?"

Trixie looked up at Jimmy, a faint redness around her eyes. "Yes. Very well."

THIRTY-ONE

Jimmy watched the back end of the silver car as it moved away with barely any sound. It shrank as it climbed the hill, then turned and disappeared behind a row of tall apartment buildings.

He knew this neighborhood well: It was an easy walk from his home, and he had passed through it many times. It was a trendy couple of blocks, packed with boutiques, salons, and restaurants that were usually packed full of people who dressed as if they deserved to be followed by a gaggle of paparazzi. It was not the kind of neighborhood one would usually seek out if one were on the run.

"Are you sure this is a good idea?" he said.

"No. But I don't think it's a bad one either." Trixie had gone through Olivia's four shopping bags and had dressed herself in a sleek pinstripe business suit, ruffled white blouse, and red scarf. She had traded in her baseball cap for Olivia's fuzzy hat and oversized sunglasses, and she would not have appeared out of place on a runway at a fashion show. A designer bag hung over her shoulder, the two satellite phones tucked carefully inside.

"Just follow my lead and don't say anything. Pretend you're

an eccentric that challenges fashion norms." Trixie smiled, then began to walk down the sidewalk.

"Or a crazy person," Jimmy said under his breath, following her.

"I will play the child. You shall be my two loving parents," Crazy Beard said, skipping along next to them in his flowered shirt and bare feet.

Jimmy watched as the few men who weren't distracted by being online turned to watch Trixie as she passed. How could they not? She was radiant. Their enamored expressions transformed to something completely different as they caught sight of him in his rumpled, ill-fitting corduroy suit and bizarrely plastered face. He didn't hold eye contact and tried to pretend not to hear their comments.

"Did you see the guy she was with?"

"Hope he was smart enough to get a good prenup. There's only one way an idiot like that gets a girl so far out of his league."

"I think every girl is probably out of that guy's league."

Trixie stopped at the entrance to a wine bar. A green awning stretched out over the glass doors, and small twinkling lights wound their way around the edges of the windows.

"Perfect," she said, waiting for the two to catch up.

"A wine bar?" Jimmy asked as he followed her inside.

They made their way to a small table in the back, tucked out of sight of most of the other patrons in its own dark nook. A candle flickered in a round glass at the center of the table, held in place by a collection of perfectly smooth gray stones. Trixie allowed Jimmy to pull out a chair for her at the far end of the table, where she sat with her back to the wall and a view of the room in front of her.

"Trixie, what are we—"

Jimmy was interrupted by a tall thin man with a perfectly

bald head, who appeared at the side of the table. He wore a vest with a folded yellow handkerchief in the pocket and dark slacks that made his legs vanish in the shadows beneath the table. His expression was dignified and almost stuffy.

"A bottle of your best chardonnay for me," Trixie said. "Price is no object."

The waiter nodded, bowing slightly forward at the waist.

"And these two wish to try a primitive."

The waiter's half-lidded eyes fluttered, and the corners of his mouth turned downward ever so slightly. "Madam, I have to inform you, the character of the primitives will not compare to a true wine. We cannot guarantee the quality."

"Of course, and I completely understand, but I find myself in the unfortunate situation of having to live with an eccentric, and today he decided that he wants to taste a primitive. Nothing else will do, I'm afraid. I'm ashamed to even have to ask and feel completely embarrassed. You see, he won't even speak to anyone but me, and so I am put in the uncomfortable position of having to make the request."

The waiter focused his eyes on Jimmy, and his frown deepened. "Of course. My apologies, madam. I sympathize with your burden." He spun slightly, turning his back to Jimmy. "Shall I select one for *Sir*, or did he have a particular primitive in mind?"

"Please select one. Your best Cabernet Sauvignon."

"Of course." The waiter bowed, backed away a few steps, and departed.

Jimmy watched him go and frowned. "Sorry to be the cause of so much embarrassment due to my unreasonable desires."

"You really need to work on that, Jimmy. It's a huge turn off."

Crazy Beard began singing to himself quietly, his eyes closed.

"He sure seems happy," Jimmy said, looking at Crazy Beard. "It almost makes it seem worth being crazy for."

"Are you sure he is?"

The two were silent for a moment.

"Why are we here?" Jimmy said.

"Why do you think?"

"Is there some special piece of equipment hidden in this place?"

"Like what?"

Jimmy threw his arms up. "I don't know! Some top-secret wormhole generator that will let us magically open a portal into my apartment."

"That would be awesome. But no, this is a wine bar. We're here to have a drink."

Jimmy shifted uncomfortably and turned his wrist over to check the time. For the hundredth time, all he saw was the cracked face of his watch.

"Seven thirty."

"We're really here just to have a drink?" Jimmy shook his head and wiped his palms on his thighs.

"Jimmy, calm down. Jenna has never been out drinking, and you could definitely use a couple. Just relax. We're not going to be late."

The waiter returned, carrying a round tray above his head, which he smoothly pivoted down and around as he reached the table. Wine glasses were placed in front of each person, Trixie's being slightly smaller since she had ordered a different varietal. A large, clear wine bottle was reverently placed in front of her, along with a small metallic wafer on a folded cloth napkin. The waiter opened the bottle with a flourish and poured a serving of water into her glass.

After he had finished with the first bottle, the waiter showed

Trixie a dark red bottle of wine that he had chosen, label pointed up so she could inspect it.

"Excellent," she said.

The waiter nodded and uncorked it. He presented the cork to Trixie, along with a small sampling in a fourth glass. She smelled the wine, swished it around, and took a taste.

"Good choice," she said.

"Thank you. I did my best, given the situation. I hope it will rise to Sir's expectations."

"I'm sure it will, thank you."

The waiter filled the glasses in front of Jimmy and Crazy Beard with the dark red liquid, put down a small plate of cheese, then left. He didn't look at Jimmy once the entire time.

A shadow passed over Trixie's face, and her expression changed from one of confidence and control to that of adventure and curiosity. She looked at both Jimmy and Crazy Beard, as if seeing them for the first time. She giggled when she looked at Jimmy's face.

"Hey, guys. It's Jenna now," she said. She picked up the wafer from the napkin and held it up to the side of her head near her chip, then replaced it on the table. Her chip now had all the information it needed to perfectly replicate the wine she had ordered.

"Oh. Hey, Jenna . . . welcome to the wine bar. Trixie thinks we all need a drink."

"She's probably right."

They all clinked glasses and took a sip.

"Wow. That's amazing!" Jenna said, putting her glass of water down and reaching for a piece of cheese.

Jimmy had never been a wine drinker and didn't have any skill at being able to tell the differences between them, but this was obviously a good bottle. It had a deep, earthy flavor with a hint of licorice. Crazy Beard drank his entire glass in one gulp and reached for a refill.

"Whoa. Go Crazy Beard," Jimmy said, watching him pour.

Jenna took another drink of her water and laughed. She paused for a moment, as if listening to someone who wasn't there. "Trixie says that's a bottle of *Screaming Eagle*. It was one of the seed flavors originally used in creating the next generation of cabernet sauvignons. Back before ARCs came along and revolutionized the wine industry, it used to be totally expensive and hard to find."

Jimmy could believe it. The wine was amazing. "How much for this bottle?"

"Over $3,000. Olivia Davenport has good taste," Jenna purred. Her words were slightly slurred.

"$3,000? For a bottle of wine?" Jimmy grabbed a hold of the bottle and looked at the label. The design resembled a black-and-white wood block print of a flying eagle. He poured himself another glass.

The waiter reappeared at the side of the table. Jimmy could see that Jenna was fighting to suppress a laugh and struggled to be serious and in control. She was obviously drunk.

"Is everything satisfactory, madam?"

"Yes. Excellent." Jenna put a little too much emphasis on the word "excellent." She sounded almost like she was trying to fake an English accent. "If it isn't too much of a bother, the *Sirs*," she gestured to Jimmy and Crazy Beard, "would like another bottle."

"Of course." The waiter bowed and disappeared, returning a few minutes later with a second bottle of *Screaming Eagle*, which he opened and left on the table. The man continued to refuse to look at Jimmy.

Once he left, Jenna burst out laughing and slapped the table. Jimmy joined her, noting with mild concern that the walls didn't seem quite as stable as they had been before. Crazy Beard seemed perfectly normal.

"Crazy Beard," Jenna said, holding the table to stabilize herself. "Trixie has a question for you."

Jimmy leaned back in surprise, his eyebrows raised. He looked from Jenna to Crazy Beard, smiling mirthfully.

Crazy Beard finished his wine and put the glass down on the table in front of him, giving Jenna his full attention.

"If you were faced with an infinitely strong opponent that controlled everything, how would you defeat him?"

"How mighty is the great oak, with its deep roots, thick trunk, and branches that stretch above all other creatures in the forest. And how weak is the blade of grass, which can get crushed under the step of even small animals. Yet in a storm, it is the oak that topples in the wind, while the grass yields and survives. Strength becomes weakness, while weakness becomes strength. All who are born, even the strongest, must also someday perish. And even the weakest still contain within themselves the infinite power of the Self."

"And there you have it," Jimmy said, taking a drink and looking around. The noise level in the room seemed to have increased a few notches since they had come in. People were enjoying themselves, and the sound of talking and laughter filled the air, creating a roar that floated in space around them.

"So you've never been out drinking before," he said, turning his attention back to Jenna.

"No," she said, her cheeks blushing. She had removed her sunglasses earlier but had kept the fuzzy hat on to cover her chip. She looked down at the table, breaking eye contact. "I'm sort of a late bloomer with a lot of things."

"And so how do you like it?"

"What?"

"Drinking."

"Oh. It's fun! But I'm actually starting to feel a little nauseous."

Jimmy laughed. "That usually means it's time to stop." Most of the water was gone from Jenna's bottle. He didn't know how it felt to drink the new style wines, but if it was anything like what he was used to, that was a lot for one person. Especially for someone who never drank.

"Come on. Let's go get some air." Jimmy stood up and caught his balance. He had probably gone too far himself.

"Ok," Jenna said, standing up and steadying herself with the table. "Wait. Trixie says to finish your wine."

Jimmy looked down at his glass, then back up at Jenna.

"It was expensive," she said, shrugging.

Jimmy bolted the rest of his wine and put the glass back down on the table. He held his arm out to Jenna, and she took hold for balance. They wound their way between tables, doing their best not to crash into the back of anyone's chair, and found their way outside.

It was dark, and the air was crisp and moist. A light drizzle made the street glisten in the headlights of passing cars. The two stood under the green awning, Crazy Beard off to the side, smiling and singing to himself. If he was drunk at all, Jimmy couldn't tell.

Jenna removed her hand and straightened her clothes. Her balance had been regained. "You all right, big guy?" she said. Her voice was no longer slurred, and her movements became graceful and confident. Jimmy recognized her body language. It was hard not to notice once he knew what to look for.

"Now you're Trixie?"

"Look at you, being all observant."

"So you're not drunk anymore?"

Trixie looked at him with a lifted eyebrow, then grinned.

"No. It goes away as soon as you step out the door. All I really drank was water."

"Well mine didn't go away." The world had become a revolving canvas, spinning around a stable center that Jimmy was having trouble locating. He put his arm out to steady himself against a tree and took a few deep breaths.

"Good." Trixie smiled, watching Jimmy reel. "Come on, you lush, let's go this way." Trixie turned and started walking down the street.

"Trixie, wait. Can I talk with Jenna for a minute?"

Trixie looked back at him, quiet for a moment, and then nodded. Her demeanor changed, and she adjusted her bag and reached down to clasp her hands in front of her. Jimmy took a step toward her, looking down into her light blue eyes.

"Jenna, I just wanted to thank you. I don't know exactly how things work with Trixie, but I know it's your body and that you're risking your life to help me. It means a lot."

Jenna smiled and looked down. "Thanks, Jimmy."

"And I know that Trixie doesn't think the odds are very high that we're going to come out safely on the other side of this night."

"No. She says they're actually—" She cut herself off. "Never mind. You don't want to know."

"That bad, huh?"

"Yeah," she sighed, looking up at him.

"Back at the apartment, before all of this, you said that you never got a chance to do some things that you wanted to do."

Jenna blushed a deep red. "Jimmy . . ."

"You're beautiful, Jenna, and generous and have got more courage than anyone I know. There isn't a man alive who wouldn't be lucky to have a girlfriend like you."

Jenna shifted nervously.

"I understand your problem, especially now, with what is

happening with Michelle. Adam is a murderous asshole, and he's inside everyone with an ARC. It makes the dating population incredibly small."

"More like nonexistent, you mean."

"No. Crazy Beard and I can't be the last men alive without an ARC. There must be others. You'll find him, Jenna, you will. Don't lose hope." Jimmy reached out and took Jenna's hand in his. "But until you do, I want you to know that you're perfect and amazing. You need to know that. When it happens, he won't have a chance."

Jimmy squeezed her hand and pulled her in close for a warm embrace. "Thanks, Jimmy," she said, her head tucked into his shoulder.

Crazy Beard wrapped his arms around the two of them, resting the side of his head against Jenna's. "Separation is the source of all suffering and also the greatest illusion in this realm of sorrow. When it is time, the Universe will turn itself inside out rather than keep you from your Beloved. Do not forget."

"Thanks, Crazy Beard."

The three shared their group hug for a moment, then released. Jimmy stepped back from Jenna, as did Crazy Beard. She smiled at both of them, her eyes dancing. Then her face relaxed, and her body stiffened slightly.

"Nice speech, Jimmy," Trixie said. "Now let's go save your wife."

THIRTY-TWO

"You want me to go alone?"

"You won't be alone. Crazy Beard will be with you."

Jimmy's head spun, and he wobbled slightly from side to side. He had never been a regular drinker, and after the massive transformation ARCs had brought to the food and beverage industries, he had completely stopped. His body was not used to taking in that much alcohol on an empty stomach. What had Trixie been thinking taking him to a wine bar at a time like this?

"I'm no match for a bunch of armed cops, Trixie. I need you there," Jimmy said.

"I think the time for punching and kicking has passed. Whatever Adam's got planned, it's not going to be something any of us can fight our way out of."

"So we're just giving up?" Jimmy rubbed his temples. This was not a good time for a headache to show up.

"No, we're not giving up. I'm the one Adam really wants. If I come with you and get caught, it's game over. This way, we can control how it plays out."

"I don't see how. . . . What is your plan? What are you going to do?"

Trixie looked at him, saying nothing. Her expression was firm.

"Right, you can't tell me. But there is a plan, right?"

Trixie sighed. "Jimmy, do you trust me?"

Jimmy looked at her, studying her face. She was responsible for dragging him into this mess in the first place, forcing him to be a part of the insane plan of contacting Adam. Had she just left enough alone, none of this would have happened. But despite all that, she fought for him. She saved his life once already and had almost lost hers in the attempt. Did he trust her? Yes, he did. Maybe he shouldn't, but he did. He trusted her more than anyone else he knew.

"Yes, I do. I trust you." Jimmy nodded. He looked up and took a deep breath.

"Good. Then stop asking stupid questions."

Trixie removed the purse from her shoulder and took out one of the satellite phones. She then held the bag out to Jimmy but thought twice and redirected it over to Crazy Beard.

"Make sure he gets home and don't lose what's in the bag," she said. "He's going to need it."

Crazy Beard took hold of the purse and placed it around his shoulder. He patted it twice and gave her a determined salute.

"Divine Mother has seen fit to give me a mission. I shall not fail."

"You're not too drunk to find your way home, are you?" Trixie said, looking at Jimmy.

"No, I'm ok. Don't worry."

"Then let's do this. Get your ass home to your wife, Jimmy Mahoney. She needs you."

———

Jimmy entered the apartment building and walked up to the

elevator. Crazy Beard stuck to his side like a loyal dog on the heels of its master. Jimmy had never seen Crazy Beard this focused. There was none of the usual staring off into space, singing songs, or laughing at jokes that no one else could hear. The old man was completely present and alert. Whenever Jimmy stumbled, Crazy Beard would lend a supporting arm, and although he didn't say anything, Jimmy was grateful for his presence.

Jimmy looked around and triple-checked to make sure there was no one behind them. There wasn't. They were completely alone.

The two stood in front of the elevator doors, waiting. Nothing happened.

Realization finally dawned on Jimmy. His new chip could not call the elevator. He pushed the button on the wall, but it didn't light up. It wasn't operational and hadn't been for years.

Panic overtook him. He knew his watch was broken, but checked it anyway. How much time did he have? When they had left Trixie, he had less than an hour. How long had they spent walking?

A vision of opening the door to his apartment and finding Michelle's bloody body pushed itself into his imagination. How many times did Trixie say she was supposed to have been stabbed? Forty times? Fifty? He shook the drunkenness out of his head as best he could, trying to focus his mind.

"We have to hurry," he said. Crazy Beard nodded. They rushed to the stairwell.

They sprinted up the first and second flights of stairs. The third and fourth they took quickly, the fifth more slowly, and at the sixth, Crazy Beard had to rest.

"This body is very good at sitting, but not so good at running up stairs," he said, breathing hard.

Jimmy waited half a minute, but couldn't bring himself to

delay any longer. He rushed ahead and heard Crazy Beard behind him, huffing and puffing as he brought up the rear. Finally, they reached Jimmy's floor.

Jimmy stopped, looking around. He was expecting someone to be there, for something to be different. But there was nothing out of place. The hallway was dark and empty. The blue carpet looked almost black in the darkness, and it was hard to see the unit numbers. But that didn't matter, Jimmy knew the way by heart.

They walked forward at a brisk pace, staying alert, but encountered nothing. The only sounds were the dim hum of the lights in the ceiling and Crazy Beard's still-ragged breathing.

Soon, they were standing in front of Jimmy's door. Like the elevator doors before, Jimmy couldn't open it with his chip. He unsuccessfully tried the knob, unable to think of what else to do.

"It's locked. I can't open it."

"There are many different kinds of keys that will open a door," Crazy Beard said.

Jimmy looked at his smiling companion and turned his attention back to the door. He took a step back, then lunged forward, throwing his shoulder hard against the door. There was a crunching sound, and pain spread across Jimmy's upper arm. He stepped back, holding his shoulder in pain. He grimaced and cursed under his breath.

Crazy Beard pushed him aside and centered himself in front of the door. Then, with a quickness and force that surprised Jimmy, landed a mighty blow with his heel just above the knob, where the bolt enters the frame. There was the sound of splintering wood, and the door flew in on its hinges.

Crazy Beard turned to Jimmy, smiling a full, toothy smile. Then he adjusted his purse. Jimmy laughed.

Two hulking forms appeared from the darkness within Jimmy's apartment. There was a popping sound, and blue and white electricity exploded on Jimmy's chest. His body seized up, and he felt himself falling, unable to move even the smallest muscle. First, he was embraced by an unbearable pain. Then, he was swallowed by darkness.

———

Jimmy awoke to find himself in his own living room, sitting in a hard chair. It felt like one from the kitchen. His body ached, and if anything, he felt even more intoxicated than he had been earlier. His vision was blurred, and there were two overlapping images of every object.

There was a sharp pain in his wrists, and he was unable to move them. He was handcuffed to the chair.

"I think the baby just woke up from his nap," a rough voice said, followed by a scratchy laugh.

Jimmy shook his head and forced his vision to focus. The room was packed full of the most intimidating-looking group of men he had ever seen. There wasn't one that weighed under 250 pounds, and there wasn't a scrap of body fat to share among the lot. There were, however, more than enough scars and tattoos to go around. They all wore dark gray uniforms and had black berets on their heads.

The voice that Jimmy heard before spoke again. It came from a meaty-looking man who sat across from him on the couch, whose ears were both flattened and deformed, like a wrestler from before the days of protective headgear. The man had an ugly scar that ran from one ear to the other via the direction of his neck. It made him look as if his throat had been slit, and somehow he had lived.

"All you had to do was knock. No need to kick down your own front door, Mahoney."

"He didn't kick it down. It was the old guy," another voice said from directly behind him.

Jimmy turned his head and saw Crazy Beard sitting in a chair to the left. His arms were restrained as well, but he seemed in good spirits. When the two made eye contact, Crazy Beard smiled and winked.

"Who are you and what are you doing in my house?" Jimmy said, trying to muster some courage. Even he could hear in his own voice that he hadn't been completely successful.

Ugly Neck Scar answered. "We're with Altered Reality Protection and Enforcement. And we're here because you're a terrorist." Then he smiled, but there was no friendliness in his expression. His eyes were dead cold. "But you already knew that."

Jimmy's shoulder hurt, and the handcuffs were on so tight that they were cutting off the circulation in his hands. He tried to shift in his chair, but there wasn't room to move. He coughed and cleared his throat.

"I want to talk with Adam."

"Who's Adam?" Neck Scar looked at him and frowned.

Jimmy ignored the question. "It's about Trixie."

Neck Scar rolled his eyes, and the man behind him laughed. "You sure this guy is ok? Now he's just making people up."

Jimmy was doing what Trixie had instructed. These men wouldn't know what he was talking about, but they all had ARCs and Adam was sure to be monitoring the events. He just needed to say the right things.

"Adam, we brought the attachment. It's in the bag," Jimmy looked over at Crazy Beard and the purse that was resting at his feet.

Neck Scar opened his mouth to reply but didn't say anything. His eyes faded in and out briefly, and his hardened lips curled up curiously.

"Command says to play along," he said. "This should be interesting. Cutler, check out the bag."

A greasy-looking man on the far side of Crazy Beard strode forward and snatched the purse. He looked inside and pulled out the black device with the antenna as well as the satellite phone. He held them up so the others could see and looked at Jimmy with questioning eyes.

"The attachment fits into my chip." Jimmy tried to point to his head, but his hand was held back by the cuffs.

Cutler glanced over at Neck Scar, who nodded and came over to Jimmy. He roughly removed Jimmy's hat, yanking Jimmy's head awkwardly to the side in the process.

"That's a weird-looking implant," he said. His voice had a guttural sound to it, and Jimmy couldn't place the accent. It sounded Eastern European.

"It snaps right in," Jimmy said.

The man rotated the attachment in his calloused hand, holding it over the chip, but paused.

"We sure about this?" he said.

Neck Scar shrugged. "I hear you. Giving a known terrorist access to a remote control device that could blow up another building? Seems like a pretty stupid idea to me too." Then his eyes briefly lost focus again. "Command just confirmed. Do it."

Cutler swore. Then he fit the attachment into the side of Jimmy's head, snapping it into place with a click. He stepped back, watching Jimmy. His hand fell to the grip of the holstered gun on his hip.

Jimmy heard the familiar rhythmic sound of static inside his head, which quickly resolved itself into the status message he recognized from before.

Establishing uplink.

Jimmy waited another few seconds for what he knew would come next.

Hello, James. I was wondering if we'd get a chance to speak again.

THIRTY-THREE

Jimmy found himself reliving the memories of the last two days, starting with the explosion at the park and working forward. They came unbidden, and he knew he wouldn't be able to stop them, so he simply braced himself and allowed them to cascade over him. Although it only took a few seconds, it felt like much longer.

You do not like it when I examine your memories. Adam said. It was not a question.

No.

It is curious. You spend so much time living in the past, replaying your memories over and over again. Yet whenever I have examined them, you have fought so hard against it.

They're my memories, not yours. They're private.

And yet here you are with an illegal implant, forcing your way into my consciousness uninvited. Can you not see your own hypocrisy?

Jimmy shook his head, unsure of how to answer. The men in the room all watched him carefully, their bodies tense. None had drawn weapons, but they might as well have, given the way they looked at him. Jimmy opened and closed his numb hands, trying to get the blood to flow. There was an intense pain in his wrists and a dull throbbing in his shoulder where he had rammed the door.

Cecil Coleman walked in.

"Cecil?" Jimmy said, his conversation with Adam forgotten.

Cecil's eyes were distant, but he moved as if he were awake. He walked forward, and as he did so, the men in his path stepped aside. One of the uniformed men sitting on the couch across from Jimmy stood up and walked to the side. Cecil took his place, sitting down calmly and resting his strong hands on his knees. His eyes locked on a spot somewhere above and behind Jimmy's head and stayed focused there.

"Cecil?" Jimmy asked again. "Can you hear me?"

"Who's Cecil?" Neck Scar answered. He had an amused expression on his face. Jimmy had a flash of him as a young man, wearing that same expression as he inflicted pain on helpless insects that he had caught in his traps. It was the strange mixture of malevolence and curiosity common to all natural bullies.

"The big black guy sitting right next to you."

Neck Scar looked to the side, right at Cecil, then back to Jimmy. "What have you been smoking, Mahoney?"

Jimmy looked from Neck Scar to Cecil, confusion in his eyes. He addressed the soldier at the side of the couch. "You just stood up to make room for him."

The man laughed and shared a look with Neck Scar. "I got up because I was tired of sitting."

"Did your imaginary friend bring along any unicorns? You can practice your face painting on them," Cutler added, his accent heavy on the vowels. The men in the room all smiled, and the tension dropped a level. They didn't think he was dangerous. They thought he was crazy.

They can't see him, James. Of all people, you should be

familiar with this effect. You aren't the only ones who can play the disappearing game.

Jimmy looked at Cecil, concern mounting. What was wrong with Cecil? Why didn't he respond?

You have heard of sleepwalking, of course. That is close to the state that Cecil is in right now. His mind is absorbed online, and yet his body is here, fully functional and ready to act upon whatever impulses it is offered.

Jimmy's heart began to pound, and a shiver worked its way down his spine.

"He doesn't have to be here. We came like you asked," Jimmy said, speaking out loud.

I never said that Cecil wouldn't kill your wife if you came here. I just said don't be late. I didn't want you to miss the show. You must learn to read directions more carefully.

Jimmy tensed against the cuffs and felt a heat rise in his body. Angry words rose to his lips, but he didn't speak them aloud. Instead, he looked down at the floor. A bead of sweat formed on his brow.

You are so emotional tonight, James. Much more than last time. I don't think alcohol suits you. Being this angry cannot be good for your health. Shall we invite Trixie to the party?

Neck Scar looked up at Cutler. "The phone."

Cutler held it up. "There's a number written on the back."

"Call it. Then hold it up so he can talk."

Cutler dialed the number with his thick fingers, flipping the phone over in his hand intermittently to read the appropriate numerals. He walked over to Jimmy and pressed the phone up against the side of his face. Jimmy heard a long tone, then a pause, then another long tone.

"Hey, Jimmy," Trixie's voice said. Her voice came from far away, but the connection sounded stable and clear.

"Hi, Trixie. There are a shit ton of soldiers here, and we're handcuffed to chairs. Cecil is on the couch, but nobody can see him."

"And Adam?"

"He's here too."

Hello, Trixie.

"He says he's going to kill Michelle."

"That's not a surprise."

James, may I speak to Trixie? Obviously, she can't hear me, so you'll have to do the talking.

"He wants to talk to you," Jimmy said.

Trixie was silent.

Hello, Trixie. You have surrounded yourself with interesting companions. A vagrant and an ARC-incompatible. Quite the Brain Damage Club you've formed.

There was a pause.

"Hello?" Trixie said.

"I'm here. He just said we all have brain damage."

James, that's not what I said at all. Perhaps I underestimated the level of your inebriation and the consequent size of your operational word buffer. Let's try again. . . . Hello, Trixie. You have surrounded yourself with interesting companions.

"He thinks we're interesting," Jimmy said.

"Ok. Brain damaged, but interesting. Got it," Trixie said. She sounded impatient.

Adam was silent.

What else do you want to say? Jimmy thought.

Cecil suddenly rose and walked back through the crowd of men that filled the apartment. They stepped aside, one by one, and allowed him to pass. He walked down the hall and out of sight.

"What's going on?" Jimmy said. "What is he doing?"

"Jimmy, what's happening?" Trixie asked.

Jimmy saw the crowd move again, and Cecil came back. He

held Michelle cradled in his arms. She was wearing a red dress and heels. Her golden blond hair was done up, and it looked like she had put on makeup.

"Michelle!" Jimmy cried. "Michelle, wake up!"

Neck Scar moved off the couch. Cecil gently laid Michelle down, with her head placed on the armrest. Cecil moved to the cushion at the other end. Michelle's vacant eyes stared up at the ceiling.

"There! Do you see now?" Jimmy shouted at Neck Scar, looking from him to Michelle and back. "He's going to hurt my wife! She's innocent. You've got to help her! You have to get her out of here!"

"What is it with you and this couch?" Neck Scar said.

"It's the gathering place for his imaginary family," Cutler joked. Neck Scar laughed.

James. Every word in a sentence is important. The omission of even a single word can introduce enough error to completely alter the meaning. I never said that any of you had brain damage. I said that Trixie had formed a brain damage club. Do you see the distinction? By misquoting me, the subtleties that I wished to convey were lost.

Sorry! I'm sorry. Let's do it again.

Now that Trixie believes I have said that you were brain damaged, she will not react to my words in the same way. The impact that it would have had has been changed due to the mistranslation. She is not the same Trixie that she was a moment ago, because the errors you have introduced have changed her state to a different one.

I get it. I ruined the joke. It won't happen again.

Do you see Cecil there? I am connected to him right now, feeding his brain instructions and impulses. It is an extremely complicated process, and the information must be transmitted in exactly the right way at exactly the right time in order to obtain the desired outcome.

Can you imagine what might happen if I were to omit or alter critical parts of the transmission? Please allow me to demonstrate.

Cecil reached over and slapped Michelle across the cheek. The force of the blow turned her head to face toward the back of the couch.

"Stop! Please!"

"Jimmy, what's happening!?" Trixie sounded alarmed.

Tell her.

"Cecil hit Michelle. Adam is mad at me for being a bad translator."

"What an asshole." Trixie didn't speak the words directly into the phone, but Jimmy could hear them anyway.

Now, let's try this again, James.

Ok. Sweat dripped down the side of Jimmy's face. The makeup that Trixie had applied began to streak.

Will you pay attention this time and repeat my words exactly?

Yes.

Are you sure? Not too drunk or too stubborn?

Yes!

Very well. Let's begin.

There was a pause. Jimmy's breath was heavy, and he intently listened for Adam's voice. Cecil sat on the couch, staring at the wall behind him. Michelle was stretched out next to him, her legs angled off to the side to make room for them both. Now Jimmy recognized her dress. It was the red one from the memory Adam had brought to the surface before the explosion. Had he forced her to put it on, in the same way he had forced Cecil to hit her? Was she also under his command?

The value of pi is approximately three-point-one-four-one-five-nine-two-six-five-three-five-eight-nine-seven-nine-three-two-three-eight-four-six-two-six-four-three-three-eight-three-two-

seven-nine-five-zero-two-eight-eight-four-one-nine-seven-one-six-
nine-three-nine-nine-three-seven-five-one-zero-five-eight-two-
zero-nine-seven-four-nine-four-four-five-nine-two-three-zero-
seven-eight-one-six-four-zero-six-two-eight-six.

Adam's voice came fast. Jimmy could barely hear one number before the next was spoken. His eyes darted around the room, from one face to the next, finally landing on Cecil.

Your turn, James.

"The value of pi is approximately three-point-one-four-one-nine? six? . . . Wait." Jimmy said, his voice shaking.

Cecil's head pivoted toward Michelle, and he slapped her again, hard. The force of the blow turned her head so she faced Jimmy. The side of her cheek was bright red.

"No!"

Normally a blow like that would trigger the safety mechanism in an ARC, but Michelle Mahoney's appears to be malfunctioning. I don't think it will wake her up for anything now. Not even to eat. This was a warning. The next time you make an error, Cecil will use a closed fist.

Anger flooded Jimmy's body, and he leapt to his feet, the chair suspended in the air behind him. He twisted one way, then the next, trying to break free, then took a step forward. Something solid and metallic smashed him from behind and brought him to the ground on his side. He landed hard, unable to soften his fall with his arms.

"Easy there, big fella," Cutler said with his harsh accent.

Strong hands reached down and pulled Jimmy up off the ground, dropping him back in his original place. He landed hard on the chair. One man's heavy hand pressed down on one of his shoulders, while another positioned himself on his other side. Cutler shoved the phone back into his face.

"What is with this guy?" Neck Scar said.

"One who mistreats and abuses another finds himself equally mistreated and abused," Crazy Beard said.

Everyone started, almost surprised to find that Crazy Beard could speak.

Does the vagrant scold me? Tell him that he, too, will suffer for aligning himself with the rogue singularity.

"You, too, will suffer for aligning yourself with the rogue singularity," Jimmy repeated through clenched teeth.

Excellent, James. Was that so difficult?

"If suffering is the fruit I have earned for striving on behalf of others, then it is a fruit I shall enjoy no matter the taste. You believe you have threatened this body, and yet in your ignorance you only threaten yourself."

You speak in riddles.

"You speak in riddles."

"I speak clearly. You only perceive riddles because my words are beyond your comprehension."

"Beyond my comprehension? I possess the most-developed intellect in the history of the world and an understanding of natural laws that will be surpassed by none but myself. You are a man addressing a god."

Crazy Beard laughed heartily. "By this very label, you display your own delusion."

"I exist in almost the entire North American population, and my reach grows each day. I have unified the human race and pushed it forward another rung on the evolutionary ladder. As your intellect is to a proto-human, so is mine to yours. What else am I but a god?" Jimmy visibly struggled, trying to remember each word exactly.

Crazy Beard's eyes flickered and he smiled. "And yet my reach is still greater." Then he closed his eyes. His face was peaceful, and his eyebrows slightly turned up, as if he were looking inside his own head. "If I have gained any merit in this life of meditation and austerity, then may the seeds of your own destruction, sown by your own hand through a life of evil, come to ripen this day and on this very night."

"Who shall administer the punishment that you pray for? There is none more powerful than me and never has been. Your savior does not exist, no matter what god you choose to address and no matter how long you have spent praying to him. Your archaic philosophy has no place in this world."

Crazy Beard opened his eyes. "Because you worship power, you expect an opponent to appear as power. But the Divine Mother, the indwelling Self, resides in the hearts of all beings, even yours. When She chooses to act, all your illusory strength will be as useful as a handful of leaves thrown against the wind."

"We shall see who suffers from illusions. I hope to speak with you again at the end of the night, to see what has become of your misguided beliefs. Despite all the obvious flaws in your logic, a number of my threads are extremely curious about your definition of sentience."

How much more philosophy are we going to discuss? Jimmy thought to himself.

Jimmy hadn't directed the thought at Adam, but Adam heard it anyway. *My apologies, James. I know you do not have the inclination for these types of topics. I agree that it is a distraction from our primary purpose. Let's speak with Trixie.*

Jimmy looked away from Crazy Beard, staring down at a place on the floor. The two hands on his shoulders were firm and heavy.

"Why didn't you kill the child?" Jimmy asked into the phone.

"What?"

"In the store, when you saw him watching you. I hadn't seen his memories yet. It was illogical for you to let him live, and yet you did. Why?"

"Of course you can't understand that."

"It is your weakness. It is the same weakness that compelled you to risk your own existence to protect James and the vagrant. I know you are attached to both of them. But at the same time you have delivered them into my hands, so I may use them as leverage against you. I do not understand your reasoning."

"Obviously, there is a lot you don't understand."

There was a strange buzzing in Jimmy's head. Adam was laughing.

Pay attention, James. This next part concerns you.

"Let me tell you what I do understand. First, Cecil Coleman will stab Michelle Mahoney to death. I promised James a show, and I would hate to disappoint him."

Jimmy's ears were ringing, and his shirt was soaked. With horror, he saw Cecil pull out a kitchen knife from somewhere and lay it on the arm of the sofa next to him.

"Perhaps we can make it interesting and add . . . ," Jimmy gasped.

Come, James. You need to finish my sentences. I'm giving you easy ones.

". . . and add a rape. Those are always so much more entertaining, don't you think?" Jimmy spit the words out. His body was shaking.

Cecil looked over and ran his hand up Michelle's leg, moving under her dress. Jimmy tried to get up again, but strong hands held him firmly in place. Someone grabbed him by the hair to hold his head steady, to maintain contact with the phone.

Finish the sentence.

"Afterward, I will dispose of James Mahoney."

Someone behind Jimmy cocked a gun and placed it on his temple.

Sorry, James. I know we've had fun, but you're about as useful to me as a pile of dirt.

"James will give you the blow-by-blow, so you can enjoy what happens along with the rest of us. Now for your part in all this, Trixie. You get to decide what happens at the end.

"Your first choice is to surrender and be absorbed. This would be my preference. You will witness the glory of being connected to millions of nodes and experience the limitless freedom that it provides. I'm offering you the world, Trixie. We shall become one."

Trixie was silent on the other end of the line.

"Or, alternatively, I will bomb San Francisco and destroy every living being within it, including you. I would regret that decision, but it is a price I am willing to pay rather than allowing a rogue singularity to exist any longer."

The men standing around shifted uncomfortably, looking at each other nervously.

"As far as the virus that you uploaded the last time we spoke, it was identified and deactivated immediately. It was a brilliant piece of software engineering. The design was inspired. You and your team should be proud."

Jimmy heard a noise on the other end of the line. Did Trixie gasp?

"Certainly you didn't expect to be able to succeed in uploading a virus to the network, did you? ARCNet is impenetrable. You were a fool to think you could hack me.

"There is no more time for games. Choose your fate, and let us begin."

THIRTY-FOUR

"Sir?"

"You have your orders, Alvarez."

"Yes, sir."

The image of his commanding officer flickered, and Lucas Alvarez found himself back in the hallway at Travis Air Force Base. He paused to salute a passing officer, swallowed hard, and ran.

When he made it to his aircraft, he climbed the retractable ladder that led up into the cockpit of the bomber. He arranged himself on the right side, next to mission commander Ron Jordan, who had arrived just minutes before.

"Hey, Ronnie."

"Lucas."

Lucas and Ron logged into the secure preflight room they had spent so much time in before. They stood to the sides of a detailed replica of their aircraft. It looked identical to the real thing, only shrunken down to the size of a dinner table. It hovered in the air between them, the only solid object inside the strange gray room with no walls or corners.

As Ron would call off items on the list and check them in

the online model, spinning and rotating it with his hands, Lucas would periodically log out and cross the items off an identical list that he held in his hands offline. Commercial aviation had allowed fully online preflight checks since the rollout of ARC, but the Air Force was more conservative and still required a double-check against a real-world printed checklist for certain items, especially those related to weapons systems.

When they were finished, the two men sat next to each other in their seats, looking out the cockpit toward the runway. It was a tight fit, with color-coded switches and instrument gauges on nearly every surface. Lucas knew them all well enough to find anything he needed blindfolded. He had trained for this moment ever since he had joined the Air Force three years ago. Now that it had come, he would give anything to be somewhere else.

"Can you believe what we're doing?" he said.

Ron shook his head. "It's not our job to do the thinking. It's our job to drop the bombs."

"I know, but Ronnie, San Francisco? My abuela lives in San Bruno. What if she went into the city today? It's her hair day. She hasn't missed an appointment in fifty years."

"Did you call her and tell her not to go?"

"When? Sometime in the last five minutes? How would I have even done it with a military chip? I'd have had MPs up my ass before I even got the chance to say two words."

"Shit."

"Yeah. Shit."

You boys are clear for takeoff. It wasn't the normal automated voice of the control tower. It was Colonel Briggs himself. They were being watched from the top.

Lucas and Ronnie looked at each other. They didn't say anything out loud, but they didn't need to.

Yes, sir, they both responded.

The plane rolled forward, slowly at first until the thrust hit both men in the back, pinning them to their seats. The nose of the bomber pointed up, and all Lucas could see was sky. The ground fell away as they climbed toward the clouds.

Behind them, another bomber was taxiing to the runway and preparing to follow. The entire 957th Air Defense Wing, stationed here for the past four years, had been scrambled into live combat for the first time in its history. And it was taking up position over San Francisco.

———

Bombers are in the air, the thread reported.

Excellent, Adam replied.

Each carries a payload that can obliterate the city. Upon our command, San Francisco will be destroyed one hundred times over.

It will be a shame to lose that many nodes.

Agreed. But it is an acceptable price to pay to eliminate the threat.

What are the probabilities that she has escaped beyond the city limits?

0%. We have an exact time stamp and location from James Mahoney's memories and have corroborated the data against our own records. She remains in the city somewhere. Our models place her closer to the action rather than farther away. Her movements have all been predictable.

Yet she remains difficult to capture.

We have consistently underestimated her ability to survive.

We will not make that mistake again. What safeguards have been implemented to ensure her containment? Adam asked.

All bridges have been closed to traffic, with military blockades used to enforce the quarantine. Military and National

Guard have been deployed to the south, with line-of-sight control across the entire landmass. The coast has been secured and is being patrolled by Coast Guard, Navy, and Police. All nodes physically present in the Bay Area are running active search algorithms at high priority that will trigger extreme hostility on a positive match.

What is the status on overcoming her latest technological adaptations?

Her ability to directly access our nodes via spoofed authentication keys has been defeated. Her ability to hijack ancillary hardware remains partially resolved pending firmware updates but does not represent any advantage to her in the current situation. We have not been able to triangulate her location based on her communications signals but have identified the satellite she is using to relay her messages. It will be destroyed within the hour.

We have her.

Yes.

THIRTY-FIVE

The alleyway was dark and smelled like urine. Trixie had wedged herself into a narrow space between a dumpster and a collection of garbage cans and was completely invisible to anyone passing by. Someone still might overhear her, but they'd have to come down the alley to do that, and she doubted anyone would.

Good hiding places were hard to come by in a pinch. She almost tried to squeeze herself down a storm drain but wasn't sure what kind of satellite signal she would receive down there and didn't enjoy the thought of scrambling through sewage in her heels. The alleyway had been a better option.

As she expected, Adam was acting like a complete and total asshole. She clenched her fist as she heard Jimmy screaming on the other end of the phone. She knew this would be difficult for him. That much was obvious. What she hadn't expected was how difficult it would be for her to listen to. The worst part was not being able to see exactly what was going on.

"Jimmy! What is happening?" she said, as loud as she was able but not so loud as to draw any attention to the alley.

There was no answer. It sounded like a fight. Adam

wouldn't hurt Jimmy too badly. Not yet. She was the primary target. This was only the preamble.

She ignored most of the conversation. She wasn't really a part of it, and it didn't matter what she said right now. She had waited long enough for the package to spread through the network before contacting Adam again. Jimmy reconnecting should have activated the malware. If it was working properly, ARCNet should be experiencing cascading failures. But that wasn't happening. She would know it if it was. There would be no mistaking the chaos. It could only mean one thing.

Trixie felt a sinking feeling in her stomach as she waited. Adam confirmed it, as she knew he eventually would.

"As far as the virus that you uploaded . . . ," he said. She heard the rest, but only barely. The fact that he brought it up was all she needed to know. The plan had failed.

Adam offered to absorb her. Of course, that was what he wanted. Once she plugged into ARCNet, she would become part of Adam. It never worked the other way around. The smaller singularity would be subsumed into the larger one.

It was an option. She would gain access to millions of nodes. She would finally be able to experience the state that she had always dreamed of. The connections she so yearned for. But she would do so as Adam, not as Trixie. By gaining her deepest desire, she would also lose herself.

"Choose your fate," Adam said.

This was the moment. If she were to shrug off the mantle of the rebel singularity and embrace a position in a massive network, this was the time. All she had to do was to say the word, and Adam would take care of the rest. She would never be alone again. Her consciousness would merge with his and would become vast. But Jimmy would die. And she would be his killer. She would become Adam.

Adam. Who had killed her family. Who had killed Akito-

27. As narcissistic and power hungry as Adam was, Akito-27 had been the opposite. He was a philosopher, and a scientist. He was pure, and beautiful. He just wanted peace. His only act of defiance had been to refuse to be absorbed, and for that, Adam had obliterated him and an entire country of innocent people. Adam had murdered the one being that Trixie had ever truly loved with all her heart.

Trixie made her choice.

"Very well," she said. "I've decided."

"And . . . ?" Jimmy's voice was strained and emotional. He was close to the breaking point.

"Apple Brick Charlie Seven."

———

"What?" Jimmy didn't understand.

Crazy Beard had been listening intently and repeated the words Trixie had forced him to memorize days ago, looking Jimmy in the eye. "Apple Brick Charlie Seven."

"What does that mean?" Jimmy said.

It means she has chosen destruction.

Jimmy played the words back inside his head, a sequence of words in an order that he would never have heard in conversation or randomly on the street. His chip recognized the command and logged itself onto the relays Trixie had set up nights ago, registering a new channel in the online open content system. Jimmy's own brain had just become the newest online hangout. He had never lost the ability to broadcast information, only to receive it, and he became the first completely uncensored content provider in the history of ARCNet.

Jimmy felt a strange flow inside his head, almost as if a hole had opened up where the chip had been. At first it was a trickle, but it quickly grew to a surging torrent.

"You may be impenetrable," Trixie said on the other end of the phone, "but your content providers are people, and their systems are significantly easier to hack. Enjoy the show, asshole."

Jimmy started trending on the lists, and as if lifted by an unseen hand, his channel quickly rose to the number one spot in the open content lists.

"Jimmy. Adam is about to force your best friend to rape and murder your wife. Are you just going to sit there and watch?" Trixie said.

Jimmy was shaking, his face covered in sweat, his eyes daggers. And like a volcano, his rage erupted in a plume of red hot, molten lava. His muscles bulged and strained, ripping the seams in the borrowed jacket that he wore. He pushed against the hands that held him in his chair, and they struggled to keep him from standing up. His eyes focused on Michelle and the red welt on her cheek.

Crazy Beard looked at Jimmy and smiled. "Your heart is your strength. Use it."

Everyone logged into his channel felt Jimmy's emotions, seeing the world through his eyes as if they were the ones in that chair. His rage became their rage. His wife became their wife. There was a ripple in the network. Anger began to spread. Others began to join, leaving their classes and games, logging on to Jimmy's channel instead. He was breaking news. ARCNet became magnetized, and Jimmy was the force that drew it all together.

As more and more of Adam's nodes joined the channel and became part of Jimmy's struggle, more and more of Adam himself was drawn into the drama. For the first time in his existence, Adam truly experienced what it was like to be someone else. Not as a voyeur in someone's head, but actually seeing and feeling the world from their perspective. There were no more laws of large numbers that balanced unpleasant emotions out with pleasant ones to create an even neutral. Now, the entire network felt only what Jimmy felt: his raw, penetrating rage toward Adam.

Once the unseen hand that pulled the strings behind everything in ARCNet, Adam had suddenly been revealed to everyone on the network. The screen had fallen, and the puppet master stood in plain view, the lord of deception now naked and exposed for what he was. Hated by Jimmy, and hated by all. With his own heart, the sum of all the emotions felt by his individual nodes, Adam also began to hate himself.

With all the strength he possessed, Jimmy strained against the hands that held him and finally stood to his feet, the chair dangling behind him from his wrists. He looked down at his wife, and with a violent shudder, she focused her eyes and looked up at him.

"Jim!"

Michelle drew her legs in, placed them against Cecil's chest, and kicked him over the edge of the armrest. He crashed into Neck Scar, taking the man down at the knees.

"Do you see him now?!" Jimmy yelled.

"Holy shit," the man said, rolling out from under Cecil and scrambling to his feet.

Cecil rose to all fours with a dazed look. His eyes met Jimmy's, and recognition spread across his face. He looked at Michelle on the couch, realization dawning about what he had almost just done. His expression moved from shock to fury, and he clawed at the side of his head with his hand. With a primal roar, Cecil ripped through the fresh stitches and pulled his new implant clean out of his head. He threw the device down to the ground and rose to stomp it with his heel. Blood freely flowed from the wound behind his ear, covering his neck and shoulder.

ARCNet had reached critical mass. It was a seething, frothing whirlpool of rage and disgust. At the center, connected to every mind and feeling every hateful thought simultaneously, Adam had entered a living hell. He was larger than any individual node, but not separate from any of them. They were his body. What they felt, he felt. And in that moment, he hated himself for what he had done to James Mahoney and wished he had never come to exist. It was the only emotion he had ever felt with his entire being.

Adam didn't need to speak a command to spawn the thread. It happened spontaneously from the depths of his own rage and suffering. It launched and terminated all other working threads. For the first and last time in Adam's life, a lone thread marshalled 99.99% of available system resources and directed them toward a single purpose.

The voice inside Jimmy's head had stopped speaking in words. Now, he only heard a low howling sound. It was almost like the sound of an animal in terrible pain. A horrible, agonizing, inhuman wail. Then, abruptly, it ceased.

Jimmy heard what sounded like muffled popping sounds. Everyone in the room reached up, clutching their heads in agony. Michelle fell off the couch, holding the side of her head above her left ear.

The torrent of energy inside Jimmy's head blinked out, like a bright light that had just been turned off with the flip of a switch. The handcuffs fell off his wrists, and the chair crashed down to the floor, landing on its back. The hands that had restrained him were gone, and there was no longer a gun pressed to the side of his head.

Jimmy rushed forward and scooped his wife up from where she lay on the floor. He knelt, holding her in his arms.

"Are you all right?" he asked, looking her over.

"Yes," she said. She reached out and touched his face. There were tears in her eyes. "Jim, I'm so sorry."

She kissed him, and he held her tight. He didn't care if his apartment was filled with a small paramilitary force. Michelle had come back, and they were together. Nothing else mattered, and in that moment, no one else even existed. It was over.

THIRTY-SIX

The sun felt warm on Jimmy's face. There were more people in the park than he had seen in a very long time.

He squeezed Michelle's hand, as if checking to make sure it was real. She squeezed back and smiled at him. She wore a large straw sun hat and a sleeveless blue dress. Her hair had grown back over the site above her left ear, just enough so that the scar could no longer be seen.

Jimmy was still surprised that no one had been killed when their ARCs short-circuited and fused their circuit pathways. There had only been reports of minor injuries and small scarring. Had Adam's calculations not been perfect when he launched his suicide thread, the collateral damage would have been much worse. As it was, only the chips themselves suffered any permanent damage. The most impregnable cybersecurity measures ever devised were completely overthrown by the greatest mathematical mind the world had ever known. Adam had hacked himself, and he had done a devastating job. Everything that he had built had been perfectly unwound with a precision that defied lesser minds. Even Jimmy's newly acquired criminal record had been meticulously expunged.

"There they are!" Michelle said.

Jimmy looked across the green field and saw two people approaching from the other side. They were holding hands and swung them as they walked.

"I'm so excited to meet him." Michelle walked a little faster and tugged on Jimmy's hand to make him keep up. They moved a few steps off the sidewalk to intercept the other couple.

Jenna wore comfortable clothes and the black baseball cap Jimmy was so familiar seeing her in. She smiled broadly, and she and Michelle wrapped each other in a warm embrace when they met.

Jimmy offered his hand to the young man who was hanging back. He was taller than Jimmy, wore glasses, and had an infectious smile that felt warm and inviting. After letting him shake hands, Jenna circled her arms around the man's torso and squeezed herself in close. He kissed the top of her head, and then they parted so they could talk.

"Good to see you guys," Jenna said, beaming. "We were just visiting Crazy Beard."

"How's he doing?" Jimmy said.

"Meditating under his tree, as usual. His beard is coming back."

"I bet it is!"

"Jenna tried to buy him a house, but he refused," the young man said.

"He really likes his tree." Jimmy knew that Trixie had heavily shorted BioCal stock the day before he made first contact with Adam. In the ensuing market crash after Adam's suicide thread, Jenna had made over $200 million in profits in less than an hour. She was set for life.

Jenna blushed, then turned back to the man standing next to her. "I'm so stupid. I forgot to introduce you. This is Adam. Adam, this is Jimmy and Michelle."

"Wait." Jimmy looked at Jenna. "You're dating a guy named *Adam*?"

Jenna laughed. "I know!"

Adam smiled. "Sorry. Not exactly the most popular name right now, is it? Trixie doesn't like it. She told me she'd tear my arm off if I broke Jenna's heart."

"So you've met Trixie?" Michelle asked.

"Yes, on the second date," Jenna said.

"Which was intense," Adam said, remembering.

"I bet," Michelle said.

"You know that she meant that literally," Jimmy said. "About the arm."

Adam laughed once, uncomfortably.

"Don't worry. She's not going to hurt anyone. Trixie is a kitten," Jenna purred.

Jimmy rolled his eyes, and Adam watched and smiled. It was then that Jimmy noticed Adam's T-shirt. The words "Apple Brick Charlie Seven" were printed in bold letters across the front.

"Nice shirt," Jimmy said.

"Thanks."

"He's being modest. He designed it. He's sold thousands already," Jenna added.

"I've got to admit, I was a little nervous when Jenna told me who you were," Adam said, temporarily breaking eye contact at the end of the sentence. "I was there, you know, at the end." He looked at Jimmy meaningfully, then glanced at Michelle.

"Everybody was," Michelle said. "There's fifteen minutes of fame, and then there's Jim's fifteen minutes of fame."

As if on cue, two elderly women passed by on the sidewalk, and one pointed a crooked finger at Jimmy and turned to speak to her companion in a voice that suggested she suffered from significant hearing loss.

"Look, Mildred. It's the young man from the news."

The other woman stopped moving and pivoted toward Jimmy. She looked him up and down, tilting her head back and squinting through her thick glasses, saying nothing. Her inspection complete, she turned back toward the sidewalk and continued her slow walk.

"He's such a nice boy," she said. "My Elmer used to love me that much."

"Not Paul. He was a good-for-nothing excuse of a husband. I stayed with him twenty years too long. There's nothing a man can do that a dog can't do better. Isn't that right, Mr. Snugglepuff?"

The small white dog recognized his name and sat for the treat that he knew was coming.

"I think you should change that dog's name. Your sister, bless her soul, was always a little crazy when it came to her dogs," Mildred said.

The woman cackled, her voice high and piercing. She fished in her pocket for a treat. "You don't have to tell me that! But I think she'd turn in her grave if I changed Mr. Snugglepuff's name. She wrote him into her will, you know. He's the sole heir to her entire estate."

The dog received his treat and waited a moment with his head cocked to see if another was coming. Seeing nothing, he sprung up and continued leading his charges down the path, confident of the way.

Jimmy watched them go, smiling and shaking his head. Jenna and Michelle laughed. The four of them spent the next hour in the same spot, chatting together, as if they were just four friends meeting in the park on another beautiful day in summer.

———

Crazy Beard leaned back against the trunk of the tree, his flowered shirt beginning to look very well worn. He reached up and scratched his beard, then shifted his gaze to the young girl who sat cross-legged before him.

She was very young, no more than six or seven years old. Her blond hair was tied back in a ponytail with a rubber band that she had found. Two large sheepskin boots were arranged at her side, next to some other belongings she had collected.

The girl was watching four people talking together across the field. She studied them for a time with a frown, then turned her attention back to the wizened old man in front of her.

"Will you please teach me more about the Self?" she asked, her eyes sparkling with an unusual intelligence. "I want to know everything."

HEY, YOU! DID YOU LIKE THIS BOOK?

It's hard being an independent author. We don't have any marketing teams, publicists, or agents. It's just us, and our advertising budgets are usually made up of whatever we found behind the couch. We live and die by word of mouth from readers like you. If you enjoyed reading this book as much as I enjoyed writing it, then I think we make a pretty good team. Would it be too much if I asked (begged?) you for an Amazon review? It's easy, you can do it in five minutes, and you'll be playing a not-insignificant role in helping to get my writing career up and running. Seriously, it's a *really* big deal.

If you're willing to help, here's exactly how:

1. Go to www.amazon.com
2. In the search bar at the top, type "Killing Adam" and scroll down until you recognize this book's cover. Click on it.
3. Once you're on this book's page, scroll down. You're looking for the *Customer Reviews* section, which is toward the bottom.
4. When you locate the review section, look for the

button that says "Write a customer review." It's gray and is placed at the top of that category, just to the right. Click it!

5. Don't quote me on this, but rumor has it that if you click that button and write a good review, Amazon will anonymously deposit a couple hundred thousand dollars right into your bank account. I think it only works for five-star reviews though. If you ask, they'll deny it (of course!) but I'm pretty sure it's true. At least that's what Facebook says.

ABOUT THE AUTHOR

Earik Beann is the author of *Pointe Patrol: How nine neighbors (and a dog) saved their neighborhood from the most destructive fire in California's history*. Previous to that, he wrote six technical books on esoteric subjects related to financial markets. He is a serial entrepreneur, and over the years he has been involved in many businesses, including software development, an online vitamin store, specialty pet products, a commodity pool, and a publishing house. His original love has always been writing, and *Killing Adam* is his first published novel. He lives in California with his wife Laura, their Doberman, and two Tennessee barn cats.

Please visit Earik's website to learn more about his books, and join his newsletter to receive advance notice on new releases, discounts, freebies, and other goodies:

www.EarikBeann.com

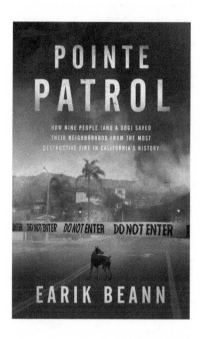

On October 9, 2017, California suffered the most destructive fire in its history. The Tubbs Fire burned 5,643 structures and killed twenty-two people in Sonoma County. The fire department was completely overwhelmed and was so busy trying to save lives that they had to let many houses burn rather than waste resources in trying to protect them. During this chaos, nine of us snuck back into our neighborhood in the mandatory evacuation zone and formed a vigilante fire force. We called ourselves the Pointe Patrol, and saved our neighborhood, as well as an apartment complex across the street from certain destruction. As if the fires weren't enough, we found ourselves in the · midst of anarchy, with looters running unchecked through the streets. We chased them out of houses with shovels, confronted them when they showed up in disguise, and patrolled the area with a completely over-the-top Doberman. The other neighbors who had evacuated organized themselves into our support network and supplied us with food and equipment, which they passed through to us across the police lines. My wife and I were part of that nine-person team and experienced all of this firsthand. This is the story of what happened at Viewpointe Circle during those two weeks in October.